Callous
HEIR

USA TODAY BESTSELLING AUTHOR
MICHELLE HEARD

Cover Designer: Sybil Wilson, PopKitty Design

Cover Model: Lochie Carey

Photographer Credit: Michelle Lancaster

TABLE OF CONTENTS

Dedication

Tayla, thank you for being the best daughter-in-law.

Songlist

Visit my playlist on *__Spotify__*

Synopsis

I made the mistake of falling for one of my brother's
friends.
As if that wasn't stupid enough, I then declared my love to
him.

Yeah, I know. Big mistake. *HUGE* mistake.
But here I am with my rejected feelings, and Noah won't
even look at me. Whenever he has to talk to me, his words
are blunt. Yet they cut deeper than any knife.

What's a girl to do when the man she loves won't give her
the time of day?

Make herself irreplaceable in his life, of course.

Noah West
More handsome than all the rest.
I loved him from deep in my bones,
But then he found out
And became all curt
And trampled my heart in the dirt.

Callous Heir

THE HEIRS
Book 5

College/New Adult series of interconnected STANDALONES.

"Life is an act of faith and an act of gamble."
— Alan Watts.

Family Tree

NOAH WEST

↓ ↓

Jaxson West   Leigh Baxter
Father   *Mother*

Godmother: Miss Sebastian

Godfather: Marcus Reed

Best Friends: Kao Reed, Hunter Chargill & Jase Reyes

CARLA REYES

↓ ↓

Julian Reyes   Jamie Truman
Father   *Mother*

Godmother: Layla Truman

Godfather: Falcon Reyes

Best friends: Forest Reyes & Aria Chargill

Noah West

More handsome than all the rest.

I loved him from deep in my bones,

But then he found out

And became all curt

And trampled my heart in the dirt.

Chapter 1

CARLA

Carla 15; Noah 20

I've watched so many motivational videos on YouTube, looking for the meaning of love. None of them could really answer me. Some say it's hormonal. Others say it's a spiritual connection with another soul. All speculations, though.

Why do I look at Noah West and feel like I might die if he doesn't love me back?

My eyes trace every inch of his body. He's all hard muscle with an air of I-don't-give-a-fuck giving him an edge.

It's that edge that attracts me. I want to leap off of it and fall... and fall... and fall into everything that's Noah West.

His dark blonde hair, hazel eyes, and the constant grin tugging at the corner of his mouth... sigh. Add that he has an IQ of between one hundred and sixty and two hundred, depending on which test you go with, and the man is damn near perfect.

But that edge. God, that edge draws me in like an addiction. I'm hooked, living for my next fix of when I'll get to lay eyes on Noah again.

Right now, I'm high on the sight of him, where he's standing near the barbeque, talking with Jase, Hunter, and Kao. Everyone's here to celebrate Jase turning twenty.

I watch as Noah laughs at something my brother Jase says. *Sigh.* He glances toward the veranda, and as he turns to walk inside, I get up and follow him.

Now's my chance to get him alone.

I watch as he goes into the restroom, and I wait at the end of the hallway with my heart stuck in my throat. I glance around, making sure there's no one else nearby. I rub my sweaty hands on my jeans and take a couple of deep breaths.

My heart thumps faster from both nerves and excitement.

When the door to the restroom opens and light spills into the hallway, I want to slap my forehead for not switching on a light. Standing like a creep in the shadows, my voice sounds like I sucked on helium as I say, "Noah. Can we talk?"

His head snaps my way, and he instantly frowns. "Why are you standing in the dark?"

I move closer and turn on the light, and then I wring my hands nervously. "Ah, there's something I want to say to you."

The frown doesn't leave his face but instead deepens. "Yeah, I think it would be better if you didn't tell me anything."

His words surprise me. "But you don't know what I was about to say."

His beautiful hazel eyes narrow on me, and then he grumbles, "Yes, I do."

Noah begins to turn away from me, and it has me blurting, "I love you."

He freezes, and he lets out an annoyed sigh. Turning back to me, he shakes his head, and his eyes lock with mine.

His expression is irritated and cold, making my heart lurch to my throat.

Then he mutters, "I'm not a pedophile. Date someone your own age."

I watch him walk away, and it takes a couple of seconds for his words to sink in. Then my world implodes, the ground opens up, everything that was perfect in my life shatters into an aching mess.

I gasp for air and fight to keep control over the devastation wreaking havoc in my heart. Darting down the hallway, I rush up the stairs so I can get to the privacy of my bedroom.

When I shut the door behind me, I fall on my bed and bury my face in my pillows. Sobs begin to shudder through me as my heart breaks.

He was so mean. God, if he doesn't feel the same, he could've at least been gentle about the whole thing.

Realizing Noah just outright rejected me without even caring about my emotions makes me feel like I don't matter at all.

I try to silence my sobs as my first love goes up in flames. It scorches all my dreams and hopes, and not even my tears can extinguish the inferno of heartbreak.

NOAH

Watching Carla run up the stairs, I feel like shit.

Fuck, why did she have to go and do that?

I've picked up on the stares filled with longing and the interest in her eyes. But shit, she's fifteen, nothing more than jailbait. Hell no, I can't even bring myself to think of her as a young woman. To me, she'll always be the little girl with pigtails and a defiant streak. I shake my head and let out a heavy breath.

I hate that I had to hurt her, but she has Reyes' blood in her veins, which means she wouldn't give up otherwise. I had to be direct, even if it was brutal.

Yeah, Carla is gorgeous, and if she was older, or I was younger… who knows. I shake my head again, stopping my thoughts dead in their tracks.

She's fifteen. A kid. A definite hell no.

I walk over to where Kao's standing with the rest of the group and say, "I'm heading back to the suite."

His eyes dart to me. "It's still early."

I force a smile to my face, hoping he doesn't pick up on the vibe that I'm upset. "Yeah, I'm beat."

"Want me to come with?" he asks.

I shake my head. "Stay and have fun. I'm just going to shower and call it a night."

"Okay." His eyes sharpen on me. "Is everything okay?"

I nod, widening my smile. "Just tired."

I say bye to the rest of the group, and with a wave, I head to my car. During the drive back to campus, Carla's shocked expression, filled with a world of heartache, is stuck in my mind.

When I walk into my room, I grab a pair of sweatpants and a t-shirt from my closet, and I go take a shower. I focus on my routine, trying to forget the evening. But the moment I drop down on my bed and my head hits the pillow, Carla and her bruised eyes are back to haunt me.

Fuck, it sucks.

I should've told one of the girls so they could comfort her. I think about texting one of them but shun the idea. It will show I care and the last thing I want to do is give Carla hope.

She'll fall for a guy her own age. I just need to avoid her until then. She'll get over me in a couple of days.

I keep reassuring myself she'll be okay and then move onto more reasons why I'm the worst possible guy for her... besides the obvious that there's a considerable age gap between us.

I'm... odd, to put it mildly. I'm a thinker, a facts person. If it can't be proven, I have no interest in it, which counts for love as well.

To me, falling in love is nothing more than a chemical reaction in your body. Love itself? It's not an emotion. I believe it's something you have to continually work at. It's being dedicated to one person. That's all there is to it.

But Carla... she believes in being swept off her feet. She believes in happily ever afters. She's a dreamer, the total opposite of me.

I let out a sigh and turn on my side.

I also need to be in control of everything in my life, especially in the bedroom. I'll fucking traumatize Carla.

I shake my head to rid myself of the thought.

I'll just keep my distance. It's the best thing to do.

Chapter 2

CARLA

Carla 18; Noah23

It's been two days since I moved into the suite at Trinity Academy, and I'm excited about the pool party they've organized for tonight.

I'm still getting used to constantly running into Noah, though. I thought I was emotionally ready to face him. I mean, it's been three years since my disastrous confession. But, like the idiot I am, I still love the guy. Don't ask me why. He sure as hell doesn't deserve a grain of affection from me.

It's infuriating to love the person you desperately want to hate.

He still treats me like I'm an annoying toddler, and I know it's only a matter of time before I lose my shit and give him a piece of my mind.

Surely, it's not a crime to love someone? Right?

I thought once we were living in the same suite, he'd at least be okay with being friends. But no, it's a full out war.

It's fine. Two can play this game, and I have no intention of losing, even though I have no idea if there can be a winner when this all comes to a head.

Letting out a sigh, I look at my reflection in the mirror. I'm wearing a white bikini with black flowers, and the black sandals make my legs look endlessly long. I'm taller than the average girl, but since my curves have filled out nicely, I don't mind the height that much.

I tie a wrap around my waist and flipping my brown curls over my shoulder, I leave my room.

I join my best friend and cousin, Aria and Forest, in the living room, so we can leave for the party.

I watch as Aria takes hold of my cousin's hand. I can't help but think there's more between them than a fake relationship that's supposed to be an act because neither of them wants to date right now. I can feel the vibes coming off them.

Shrugging the thoughts away as we walk toward the pool house, a smile forms around my mouth. My friends will be okay. Tonight I just want to have fun.

The instant I step inside, I feel eyes on me. I take a deep breath as three guys approach me. I don't mind the attention, but nothing will come of it. It's only ever been Noah for me. All the other guys end up annoying me during the flirting stage, so I cut things short before they can even ask me out on a date.

"Looking hot, Carla," Adam, who's a senior at Trinity, says. His eyes slowly sweep up my body, and it makes me feel like a two-dollar hooker.

I narrow my gaze at him, not appreciating the way he's checking me out. "Stop looking at me as if I'm for sale."

I hear Aria shriek and glance toward the pool, in time to see Noah throwing her into the air before she plunges back into the water.

There's a jealous stab in my chest.

Why can't he be like that with me? Instead, he treats me as if I have some disease.

Ignoring Adam and his friends, I walk to a lounge chair and take a seat.

The pool fills up quickly with half-dressed bodies, and soon water is splashing everywhere.

"Noah," I hear Julianne's annoyingly high-pitched voice, and my gaze searches for them.

I watch as she places her hand on his arm, and when he pulls away from her, a smile forms around my lips. Glad to see I'm not the only one he's rejecting. My eyes drift over his chest and his abs.

Ugh, why is he so hot?

Julianne pouts, and I wish I could hear what they're saying to each other. Noah looks annoyed, and walking away from her, he dives back into the pool.

"Hey, cuz," Fallon says with a smile as she comes to sit by me.

Surprised to see her, I reply, "Hey, I didn't know you were coming."

"I'm just showing my face, and then I'm heading home," she explains. Her eyes dart to someone behind me, and she grins, "Hey, Noah."

I instantly freeze, and I try, I really try, but I can't stop myself from looking over my shoulder. Noah's busy patting drops from his chest with a towel.

Damn, I wish I was that towel.

"Hi," he smiles at Fallon. "Where's Kao?"

Kao's engaged to my cousin, and he's also Noah's best friend.

"He stopped by his parents' place after work. He's probably still there." Fallon climbs to her feet, and her eyes settle on me. "I'm going to hit the road. I'll see you tomorrow."

21

I get up and give her a hug.

Fallon starts to walk away but smiles at Noah. "We're seeing you this weekend for the big move, right?"

"Yeah," he replies, and for a second, his eyes lock on me before he turns around and walks away.

Every time he's friendly with one of the other girls in our group, it digs a chunk of my heart out.

God, I want to hate him. Damn, I'll even settle for intensely disliking him.

NOAH

It's hard to adjust to Kao not being at Trinity anymore. Seeing Fallon lessened the loneliness, though.

Damn, I miss my best friend.

Because I'm doing two degrees instead of one like Kao did, I'm stuck at the academy for an extra year.

I glance around at the other students, and there's not one I remotely want to be friends with. I don't have the patience for meaningless conversations.

Letting out a sigh, I decide to take one last dip in the pool before returning to the suite. I dive into the water, and coming up on the other side of the pool, I hoist myself out.

"Oh, look what the cat dragged in," I hear Carla's voice.

My gaze sweeps over her, and taking in the scant pieces of fabric barely covering her sexy-as-fuck body, I tilt my head and ask, "Did you only get half your pocket money this month, and that's why you couldn't afford the other half of that bathing suit?"

Carla's eyes narrow on me, but then she shakes her head, and impersonating *Buzz Lightyear* from *Toy Story*, she says, "You are a sad, strange little man, and you have my pity."

This girl... Fuck she annoys the living hell out of me with her impersonations.

Since she declared her love to me three years ago, I've done my best to stay away from her. I can't even bring myself to think of her as anything more than a kid. Yeah, she might be all long legs, curves, and a beautiful face, but still, she'll always be a kid to me.

I take a step closer to her and say, "Don't you think it's time you grow up, little girl? You're in the adult world now."

"God, help me," Carla hisses, anger making her features tighten.

Forest grabs hold of her arm, and his eyes lock on mine. "That's enough."

If there's one thing I've learned, it's not to take on the Reyes' family. Holding up my hands, I shoot a glare at Carla so she'll know to back off, then I turn and walk away.

God, I miss the old group.

I keep walking until I'm in the suite, and the emptiness makes me feel antsy. I take a shower, and pulling on a pair of sweatpants and a t-shirt, I decide to chill in the living room.

I grab my phone from my desk and walk out of my room. Plopping down on the couch, I turn on the TV and go to *CNN*.

Opening messenger, I shoot my mom a text.

N: Bedtime story?

Knowing Mom might be busy at the hospital, I rest my phone on my thigh and focus on the news. I get lost in what's happening around the world until Forest and Aria walk into the suite. They disappear down the hallway.

Checking my phone, I see a message from Mom.

M: Hi, baby. I had a patient today with an infundibular ventricular septal defect. It's basically a

24

dangerous hole in the aortic valve. It's a common congenital heart disease, and I had to perform an early surgical intervention to prevent aortic regurgitation progression.

I read the rest of her message, a smile forming around my lips. My mom's the best cardiothoracic surgeon in the states, and her medical journal entries have been my bedtime stories since I can remember.

"Watching porn?" Carla suddenly asks, making my head snap up. She takes a bottle of water from the fridge.

Instantly annoyed, I ask, "Shouldn't you be in bed?"

"Ooooh… wanna tuck me in?" she asks, the corner of her mouth lifting before she takes a sip.

Oh, little girl, you wouldn't be able to handle me if I were to tuck you in.

"Night, Carla," I mutter as I turn off the TV and get up.

I only reach the hallway when Carla makes a sputtering sound. My head snaps toward her, and seeing that she's choking on water, I walk to her and slap her back.

She tries to take a breath, but it sounds like she's being strangled. I move in front of her and framing her face, I stare into her watery eyes. "Breathe through your nose." She manages to get some air in. "Again."

Her hand clamps on my forearm, and the sight of a tear spilling over her cheek makes a weird emotion ripple through me.

It sounds painful as she drags in air, and then she begins to cough. I move to her side and rub a hand over her back. "It's okay."

It takes her a couple of minutes to catch her breath, and then she mutters, "Death by water. Who would've thought?"

Tilting my head, I ask, "Are you okay?"

Her eyebrow pops up, and I instantly regret asking the question.

She clears her throat, but her voice is still raspy as she asks, "Wow, is that a note of concern I heard?"

"Nope." Letting go of her, I head down the hallway.

"Too late, Noah. I know you care, or you wouldn't have asked if I'm okay."

Turning back to her, I say, "No, Carla. It's just the humane thing to ask after someone chokes."

She walks toward me, a daring light in her eyes. "Yeah? So you feel nothing for me? Is that what you're saying?"

"We move in the same circle, and you're Jase's little sister," I remind her. "Stop reading more into every single thing I do. You make me uncomfortable."

26

"How do I do that?" she asks, crossing her arms over her chest.

"You're a kid."

Her gaze narrows on me. "I'm eighteen. Stop calling me a kid or a little girl. It's demeaning."

Leaning a little forward, I say, "You'll always be a kid to me. Get that?"

She takes a step closer to me, and lifting her chin, she chuckles. "It's only a matter of time, Noah. If you haven't realized yet, I don't give up easily."

Shaking my head, I glance up at the ceiling before I decide this conversation is over. I turn away from her and walk to my room, frustrated as hell.

Chapter 3

CARLA

Forest and Aria seem to be caught in their own little bubble, and it makes me feel a bit lost. I always hung out with them, but since we started at Trinity, I've been pretty much on my own.

Sure there are lots of girls here I can befriend, but the problem with being a Reyes is that you never know if someone is your friend because they genuinely like you or because they want to up their status.

Sitting alone in the restaurant, I let out a sigh. When Fallon, Mila, and Hana, my other roommates, walk into the establishment, a smile instantly forms around my mouth.

They each take a seat, then I say, "You're a sight for sore eyes."

Fallon frowns at me. "Why? What happened?"

I shrug. "I'm just struggling to find my place here. Forest and Aria are so busy with their fake relationship, it doesn't leave much time for them to hang out with me."

Mila, who's Jase's girlfriend, and hopefully my future sister-in-law, places her hand on my arm. "You can hang with me any time."

Jade smiles at me. "Yeah, what she said."

Fallon scoots closer and places her arm around me. "Sorry, hon. I should've made more of an effort."

I shake my head. "It's just weird adjusting to how things work here."

Mila picks up a menu, then asks, "What are we eating?"

Without looking at the selection of meals, Fallon answers, "I'm having a salmon salad."

"I want steak," Jade murmurs.

My lips curve up, and having company for lunch makes me feel a hell of a lot better than I did a couple of minutes ago.

A waiter comes, and when Fallon places her order, I say, "I'll have the same as her, with an orange juice." I can't handle the fizzy taste of soda. It makes my teeth feel like sandpaper has been rubbed over them.

Suddenly Noah sits down next to Fallon, muttering, "Ladies." He pulls a menu closer and quickly glances over it, then he tells the waiter, "A cheeseburger with extra cheese and…" he looks at the drink selection, "Cranberry juice, please."

"Ugh… I miss Hunter," Jade says. "I keep expecting him to appear at any moment."

"Yeah, I'm driving Kao insane with texts," Fallon chuckles.

"He loves all the attention," Noah tells her, and he even gives her a warm smile.

Damn, that jealous twinge.

Fallon's gaze snaps to Noah. "Yeah? Did he tell you that?"

Noah nods, and taking his phone from his pocket, he shows Fallon a message which makes her laugh.

Our food comes, and my eyebrow pops up when I watch Fallon take the garnish from Noah's plate.

Why can Noah be so close with my cousin, but with me, he's worse than the Grinch?

'Because she's not in love with him. He can be comfortable with her,' my mind answers the question, and it leaves me feeling torn.

Should I give up? Should I try to find a way to love Noah as a friend? It would be better to have any kind of relationship with him, instead of him running at the sight of me.

It's not the first time I've considered giving up on Noah. I would try for a week, but then I'd see him, and all

30

my resolutions would go up in smoke. But that was before we had to live in the same suite. Now that we're continually running into each other, my unrequited love is becoming a problem for both of us.

Since Noah rejected me the first time, the cracks covering my heart keep tearing open every time I consider giving up. How do you let go of the one thing you want more than your next breath?

I focus my attention on my meal, glad it's nothing big because my appetite is missing in action.

As soon as I'm done, I wipe my mouth and get up from the chair. "Catch you all later." Walking away, I impersonate *Dori* from *Finding Nemo*, "When life gets you down, you know what you gotta do? Just keep swimming." I let out a chuckle, and heading out of the restaurant, I murmur, "Just keep swimming. Just keep swimming."

Yeah, I'll just have to do my best to get over Noah. Whether it's something I can actually do, remains to be seen.

NOAH

I'm not the type to party. Just like my best friend Kao, I'd rather stay in the shadows. It saves me from having to interact with people. It's not that I'm a hermit like Kao, but rather that I struggle to communicate. I don't understand people, and they don't get me.

When Forest mentions they're staying in, I figure I have to try and be social with them, seeing as we'll be future business partners. I might not get along with Carla, but damn, I'll have to work with her one day.

I have to admit, she hasn't given me any shit since Tuesday night.

"What game are we playing?" Forest asks.

Remembering all the games Jase had us playing, I mention, "We can play fear pong."

Aria glances at me, and she asks, "Fear pong?"

I quickly explain, "Yeah, we write dares on the bottom of the cups, and you either do the dare or drink. The winning team wins two hundred dollars."

"Team?" Carla asks, her eyes locking on me. She lets out a chuckle. "God, this is going to be priceless."

Shaking my head, I ask, "Enlighten me as to why?"

Then she smirks at me. "You and I. We're on a team."

Shit. I should've thought of that.

Hoping this doesn't bite me in the ass, I mutter, "Fuck."

The girls leave to change into comfortable clothes, and the second we're alone, Forest asks, "Will the two of you manage to not kill each other tonight?"

I let out a chuckle to set him at ease. "Yeah, don't worry. I'll take it easy on her."

While Forest goes to his room to change, I grab the solo cups and whiskey bottle from the cupboard.

Lord knows I'm going to need alcohol to get through tonight.

When everyone is ready, we take our places on opposite sides of the island in the kitchen. The girls check something on their phones, and when they start writing the dares under the solo cups, I begin to worry.

Carla better not write dares like kiss your partner or this game is over.

Forest reads one of the dares, "Tell the opposing team about a dirty fantasy you would never actually do in real life? Seriously?"

Carla shrugs. "We got the dares online."

Unable to resist, I mutter, "I have a dirty fantasy. It involves tape and Carla's mouth."

An image involving Carla, rope, and tape flashes through my mind, causing an unexpected wave of heat to rush through me.

What the fuck was that?

I clear my throat as Forest snorts. Pouring myself some whiskey, and as I take a sip, Carla looks at me. "Yeah? You don't want to hear mine."

Finally, something we can agree on.

Lifting my chin, I pin her with a stare. "Let me hear it."

"It involves you having three Adam's apples," she sasses me.

It actually makes the corner of my mouth lift. I'd rather take Carla's threats over her flirting with me.

Carla gets to go first, and she sinks the ball, making my eyebrow lift. She lets out a happy shriek next to me.

Forest reads the dare then asks, "So, I have to do whatever Aria tells me?"

"Pretty much," I murmur. "Or you can drink."

Forest takes the dare, and when he throws the ball, it misses. "What now?"

"You both drink," Carla grins at them. They each down a shot of whiskey.

When it's my turn, I sink the ball. Aria checks the dare, and then she lets out a snort of laughter. "Act out your three favorite sex positions, roles reversed."

I let out a bark of laughter. "This is going to be good." When Aria begins to act out the positions, I crack up with laughter. It's funny because she's half the size of Forest.

Carla wipes tears from her face. "I wish I could've recorded that. Best ever."

Aria gets the ball in, and she and Forest high five each other.

I pick up the cup and read the dare. "Aww, fuck," I mutter. "Let your partner cut off your shirt." I glance at Forest and Aria. "I fucking love this shirt."

Carla surprises me by saying, "I'll let you change into one you're not too fond of."

Not giving her a second to change her mind, I say, "Be right back." I rush to my room and change into a plain white shirt. When I get back to the kitchen, I give Carla a look of warning. "Don't stab me."

Maybe this isn't such a good idea. Carla might just take the chance and bury the scissors in my gut.

"Damn, there you go and ruin it for me," Carla mutters while she gets the scissors from a drawer.

There's a mysterious gleam in her eyes, which I don't like one bit. I watch her closely as she takes hold of my shirt, and then she cuts right through it.

I'm just about to let out a sigh of relief when she sets the scissors down, but then she looks up at me and moving her hands under the fabric, her palms glide over my skin as she pushes the shirt off.

An unwelcome burst of desire courses through my body, and reaching for my drink, I take a huge gulp.

Don't go there, Noah. Carla is way too innocent.

Feeling uncomfortable, I try to focus on the game, but then Forest gets a ball in one of the cups, and when a smile spreads over Carla's face, I know I'm in deep shit.

I hold my breath while I wait for her to read the dare. "Fake an orgasm with your partner."

At least it's not a kiss or anything physical we have to act out.

Or so I thought.

Carla turns to me, and she comes to place her hand on my shoulder. She lifts herself on her toes, and when I feel her breath flutter over my ear, my body reacts in a way I never expected it to. My cock goes from minding his own business to taking notice of Carla's body so close to mine.

36

Then she lets out a moan that has my heartbeat speeding up, "God, Noah... Harder."

Fuck.

"Ah... ah... yes, right there." Carla presses her body tightly against mine, and my hand instantly grabs hold of her hip.

I can feel her body's heat through our clothes. Every curve presses against me, and it confuses the hell out of me because I'm not into inexperienced women. Especially not in the bedroom.

She lets out a breathy moan, "Ah... God, I'm going to come..."

Images of Carla in the bikini that didn't cover much, begin to flash through my mind, and then it leads straight to flashes of her quivering on my bed.

Yes... Fuck, Noah." My mouth dries up, and I swallow as my cock reacts, hardening at the speed of light.

Fuck. This is Carla. Don't go there.

And then she lets out a fucking cry that has my cock straining against the zipper to get to her and my hands itching to explore her curves. There's a burst of desire to dominate her, and I struggle to breathe through the overwhelming feeling as Carla pulls back.

She gives me an I-told-you-so look, then says, "You can wipe the drool off your mouth. The show's over."

I suck in a deep breath, hoping none of the emotions are showing on my face. Needing some distance from Carla, I say, "I think we should take a break and order in."

"Yeah, sure," Forest agrees. He grabs a menu. "What are you all in the mood for?"

"Noah wants a cold shower," Carla taunts me, and I worry that she felt my cock hardening while she was pressed up against me.

Wanting to distract everyone and get back at Carla, I open the freezer, and taking ice from it, I turn to her. Her eyes instantly widen, and she tries to dart away, but I grab hold of her arm and yank her back to me. Her soft scent fills my lungs, and there's a crackle of electricity between us. Dropping the ice down the back of her shirt, I whisper close to her ear, "This will help you cool down."

"Oh God!" Carla shrieks. She begins to shake and wiggle her body to get rid of the ice.

Everyone laughs, and it has me chuckling. "It looked like you were overheating, so I thought I'd help out." Wanting to fuck with her, I wink at her before taking the menu from Forest. "Should we get platters?"

Chapter 4

NOAH

I could've graduated years ago with my high IQ, but my parents wanted me to have a normal upbringing. For the first time in my life, I regret not fighting them on it.

If I had finished my studies sooner, I wouldn't have to share a suite with Carla now.

After last night's game, I've been sneaking in and out of the suite like a damn burglar, doing my best not to run into Carla. Figuring out what I'm feeling is like trying to solve the mystery of life itself. It's damn near impossible.

I was awake half the night, replaying what happened in the kitchen. Even though Carla is beautiful, I've never felt an attraction toward her... until she fucking touched me.

It's probably just a physical reaction from having a female body pressed against mine. Right? Then again, I've never had a strong response like that to a girl before.

What really bothers you, Noah?

The fact that Carla made you feel something or the fact that you've never felt something so intense before?

I've tried dating a couple of times, but it's not something I'm cut out for.

Luckily I'm helping Kao drive all their stuff to the new house while Carla's helping Fallon unpack everything.

"Remind me again why you didn't hire a moving company?" I ask Kao as I'm busy driving us back to his house.

"Fallon and I want to do this ourselves. It's part of the whole experience," Kao explains.

"What experience? Working yourself to death?" I mutter as I pull up the driveway. They bought a ranch-style house, much to my surprise. I always thought Fallon would want a mansion like the one she grew up in.

Kao reaches for the door but stops when I say, "Can we talk?"

He relaxes back in the seat and looks at me. "Sure. What's up?"

I take a deep breath, then mutter, "Carla."

A smile begins to form around his lips. "What about Carla?"

Scratching the back of my head, I let out a sigh. "Things are weird. I don't understand it."

"How weird?" Kao asks his full attention now on me. "What happened?"

He knows Carla told me she loves me, and back then, he agreed I did the right thing.

"She's not giving up," I tell him. "Things have been volatile between us. Last night we played fear pong, and she had to act out dares with me." I shake my head, then admit, "I felt something... with her."

"Felt what?" Kao asks. "Tingles, a fluttering, desire? You need to be more specific here."

"Desire and something else I don't... It was..." I try to think of a word. "It was warm, almost like compassion?"

"Could it be you're interested in her?" Kao turns in his seat, so he's facing me. "You don't have to dissect every single thing in life. I know it's your first instinct, but you'll miss out on half of life if you do that." He places his hand on my shoulder. "If you're attracted to her, I say give it a chance. Look at Fallon and me. We're opposites, and it works for us."

I lock eyes with Kao, "Carla and I aren't opposites. We're fucking light years away from each other, and she's five years younger than me. She's a kid." Thinking she's so much younger than me doesn't bring me the same wave of apprehension and aversion it always has in the past.

"Noah,". Kao squeezes my shoulder, "it's time you admit Carla isn't a kid anymore. Three years ago, it would've been wrong, but now it's a different story. She's had time to grow up."

"Mentally, I know she's an adult, but," I tap against my heart, "in here, it feels wrong. As if I'll be taking advantage of a teenage girl's innocent crush."

"It's only been a week. You don't have to find all the answers right now, although I know it will probably drive you insane if you don't solve every damn thing life throws your way." Kao takes a breath, then continues, "If you want my advice, just hang out with her. If the feelings continue to grow, then go for it. If you don't fall in love with her, the worst that can happen is you'll become friends. You can't keep treating her like an annoying kid. That shit is going to get you on the wrong side of Jase."

Kao's right. It's only a matter of time before this thing starts to affect everyone around us, and I'm not one for drama.

"What if I'm friendly with Carla, and she takes it the wrong way?" I voice my biggest worry.

"Then you sit her down and have a conversation with her. Tell her how you feel, and respect how she feels. I think it's about time that conversation happened. You can't just swat Carla away as if she's a fly. She's one of us and deserves more than that."

"Me… have a conversation?" I let out a chuckle. "You know I suck at talking to people."

"Pretend you're talking to me," Kao says.

I give him a scowl. "Yeah, I don't think that's going to work. You understand me."

"Just try, Noah. If you can't communicate with her and things get bad, then I'll talk to her. Okay?"

I let out a sigh. "Yeah, okay." Giving Kao a smile, I say, "Thanks for listening."

"Always." Kao nods his head toward the house. "Let's get in there before Fallon asks where we are. She has us on a tight schedule."

I let out a burst of laughter as we climb out of the car, and we each grab a box from the U-haul trailer.

Walking toward the house, I decide to take Kao's advice. After all, he is the one with a successful relationship. I'll be friendly with Carla and see where things go. If I keep feeling awkward, I'll tell her I only want to be friends. But if these emotions keep growing… My mind comes to a screeching halt.

One step at a time, Noah. First, try to be friends with her.

When we enter the living room, we find the girls sitting amongst boxes. Carla looks up, and the second her gaze lands on me, she impersonates a scene from *Tangled*, "Whoa! Somebody get me a glass. Cause I just found me a tall drink of water."

Even I have to admit she's really good with doing impersonations. I let out a chuckle, and shaking my head, I place the box by the others.

CARLA

What just happened?

My mouth drops open, and stunned, I stare at the smile on Noah's face.

Where's the scowl? Where's the glare of death?

Maybe he's just being nice because everyone else is here?

Yeah, that's probably it. Don't read anything into a simple smile.

I continue to unwrap Fallon's collection of gemstones, then I ask, "Where are you going to put all of these?"

"I have a crystal vase somewhere. I'll just chuck them all in there."

"This vase?" Hana, who's Fallon's best friend, says as she holds it up.

"Yeah, pass it to Carla."

I take the vase and carefully drop the gemstones inside.

Kao comes back into the living room with Noah right behind him, and they set down the boxes in their arms. Then Kao's gaze rests lovingly on Fallon. "Babe, you still want me to go get pizzas and beer for when we're done unpacking?"

"Yes." She climbs to her feet and goes to give him a kiss. "We'll be done in an hour."

Kao presses another kiss to her lips. "Anything else we can get while we're out?"

"Maybe some wine?" I ask. "I struggle with beer."

"What kind?" Noah asks, and again I can only stare. He tilts his head. "Carla, which wine do you like?"

"Ahh…" I gape like a fish because he's actually talking to me of his own free will. I finally manage to gather my shocked self enough to answer, "Semi-sweet white, please."

When he nods, I ask, "You're not going to give me hell for being too young to drink?"

Noah shrugs. "It's not my place. Besides, it's no different than Fallon having a beer."

Whoaaaaa? What the…? Huh?

I'm still stunned out of my mind when the guys leave.

"Are you okay?" Fallon suddenly asks, yanking me out of my thoughts.

"Yeah, just confused. Noah's never nice to me."

"What do you mean he's never nice to you?" she asks, a frown forming on her forehead.

It's just us girls, and deciding to tell them what happened three years ago, I say, "I had a crush on Noah way back, and he shot me down. Since then, we've been… let's just say Noah does his best to keep me at a distance."

"Why didn't any of us know this?" Fallon asks, glancing at Hana, Jade, and Mila.

I shrug. "I wasn't about to advertise my being rejected to the whole world. It was embarrassing enough when it happened."

Fallon's frown deepens. "But we're not the whole world."

"I know." I shrug again. "It's over and done with."

"Are you still in love with him?" Mila asks.

With Mila being Noah's cousin, I shake my head and lie, "Nah, I got over being in love with him a couple of years back."

Aria and Forest finally walk in when we're almost done with all the work. It's on the tip of my tongue to ask them where they've been, but I decide not to. If they wanted to tell me what's going on with them and why they're keeping their distance from me, then they would've.

We stack all the empty boxes in the U-haul Kao and Noah left here, then start to clean the house. Mila and Jade dust everything while Hana mops the floor.

Walking into the kitchen, I see Forest and Aria washing and drying the dishes.

"Hey," I murmur as I begin to help Fallon pack them away.

Aria grins at me. "Hey." I also get a smile from Forest, and it makes me wonder if I'm not just oversensitive.

We're busy packing away the last of the plates when Fallon says, "Leave those out for the pizza." She places glasses for the beer and wine next to it, then looks at me and asks, "Can you help me with the bedding?"

"Sure." I follow her to the first bedroom, and we each grab a side of the sheet and pull it over the mattress.

Wanting to make conversation, I ask, "How does it feel to own your own home?"

"A little surreal." Fallon glances around the guest room. "It's exciting and emotional."

She takes a shaky breath, which has me moving closer to give her a hug. "You deserve this with Kao."

"Thanks." She smiles and takes a deep breath. "And thank you for being here today. I really appreciate it."

"I wouldn't miss it for anything."

We move to the next room, and by the time we're busy with the main bedroom, it feels like my back's about to break in half.

Straightening up, I place my hands on my lower back and stretch. "God, my back. I feel eighty years old."

"I hear you," Fallon agrees.

Just then, Noah peeks into the room. "Are you almost done? The pizza's here."

"Just in time," Fallon grins, walking past Noah and down the hallway.

I keep rubbing my back as I follow after her.

"What's wrong?" Noah asks from behind me.

I glance over my shoulder. "Nothing. Why?"

He gestures to me. "You're rubbing your back."

"Oh." I wave a hand. "Pfft, just sore from bending over while making the beds."

"Hold up," he says.

When I stop walking, Noah's arms come around me from behind. My eyebrows disappear into my hairline as he pulls me back against his chest, and then he lifts me off my feet, and I hear a cracking sound.

"Oh, God… Noah," I groan from relief.

I don't even have time to absorb the feel of having his arms around me because he instantly sets me down and steps back.

Turning around, I grin at him. "Thanks. It feels much better." Then I see the startled look on his face, and it makes my heartbeat speed up for some reason.

Not wanting this weird peace treaty to end, I say, "You should've gone into the medical field like your mom. You have a healing touch."

Spinning around, I walk away from him.

Yeah, don't rock the boat, Carla. Enjoy the cease-fire cause it won't last forever.

Chapter 5

NOAH

I follow Carla into the kitchen, still trying to process the burst of desire I felt when she groaned.

Yeah, whether I like it or not, something is happening… between us. I pull a face, not comfortable with the idea.

Just be friends with her, Noah.

Carla inspects the bottle of wine, then says, "Oh, I love this wine. Thanks, guys."

Taking hold of the bottle, I open it for her and pour some in a glass. When I shift the glass to where she's standing, she watches me with wide eyes.

"Do you want ice?" I ask, figuring that's what the look is for.

"Uh… No. I'm good, thanks." She picks up the glass and takes a sip, her eyes still locked on me.

I shrug and closing the bottle, I set it aside. I reach for a plate and grab two slices of pizza. Leaning back against one of the counters, my gaze drifts over all my friends, and seeing them happy makes a smile tug at the corner of my lips.

"Wow," Hana suddenly says. "Can you all believe how far we've come over the past year? I mean, we're standing in Kao and Fallon's home."

"Yeah, it's been quite some year," Mila murmurs.

"Where's Jase?" I ask. "And Hunter?"

"Oh, they're working," Jade answers. She glances at her watch. "They should be here at seven."

A slight frown forms on my face when I notice Carla standing to the side, deep in thought. Carla is like Fallon in many ways, and seeing her not taking part in the conversation is unlike her.

Before I can think it through, I move closer and lean back against the cupboard by her. I cross my arms over my chest and leaning down a little, I ask, "Are you okay?"

Her eyes widen on me again. "Ahh… yeah?" She shakes her head. "Not to ruin things, but why are you talking to me?"

I shake my head. "What do you mean?"

"You never talk to me unless you really have to," she explains.

I shrug and glance over the kitchen. "I'm trying the friends thing, seeing as we're now living together. Fighting with you is exhausting."

"Oh… okay." She relaxes and takes a sip of her wine.

My gaze drops to her, and I wait for her to comment more on what I just told her, but when she keeps quiet, I ask, "What? You have nothing to say?"

Shaking her head, she smiles at me. "Hell no. I'm taking the olive branch." Carla grins, then does an impersonation of *Edna* from *The Incredibles*, "I never look back, darling. It distracts from the now."

I let out a chuckle, then mutter, "Good." When she takes another sip of her wine, I say, "You should eat something."

Her eyebrow pops up, and she almost says something but then presses her lips tightly together. It looks like it's killing her to keep quiet.

"Let it out before you stop breathing," I mutter.

She begins to chuckle. "Careful, Noah. It's seriously starting to sound like you care."

I shake my head and pushing away from the counter, I walk to where Kao is shoving a piece of pizza in his mouth.

When everyone's done eating, I help Kao clean up while the girls hang out in the living room.

"Things seem to be going okay with Carla," he mentions as he hands me a plate to dry.

"Yeah. It's weird but okay," I admit.

"It's a step forward, though," he says.

"That remains to be seen," I mutter.

Jase comes into the kitchen. "Hey, guys."

"Hi," I reply as I place the last plate in the cupboard.

"Why are you working on a Saturday?" Kao asks him.

"We're busy with a big contract," Jase explains. He grabs a beer from the fridge and gulps some down, then he asks Kao, "Are you going to show me around?"

I hang the towel on a hook so it can dry and walk to the living room. Jade is kissing Hunter as if she hasn't seen him for months.

My gaze lands on Forest and Aria, where they look like a lovesick couple.

Yeah, fake relationship, my ass.

There's a seat open next to Carla, and figuring it's safe enough with everyone here, I drop down next to her. Her eyes are on her best friends, and there's a slight frown on her forehead. She tilts her head closer to me and whispers, "Is it just my imagination, or do they look in love?"

My eyes go back to Forest and Aria. "Nope, not your imagination."

"Yeah, that's what I thought," she murmurs.

I can't tell if she's happy for them or not, so I ask, "Do you have a problem with them dating?"

Carla turns her eyes to mine. "No, I just hate when people hide things from me." She shrugs. "If they're happy with each other, that's all that matters." Her gaze goes back to them. "They've been best friends forever. I really think they could make a success of a relationship. They're already committed to each other."

Her words hit me deeper than I expected, and I ask, "Do you really think that's all it takes?"

"Of course." She frowns at me. "Don't you?"

"Yeah, I'm just surprised you think so, too," I reply.

Her frown deepens. "What do you mean by that?"

"Just," I turn my body a little towards hers. "I would've thought you'd believe in true love."

"What? Like falling madly in love and it staying that way forever?" she asks. When I nod, she chuckles, "Come on, Noah, we both know that's only the initial hormones going into overdrive. When the honeymoon phase is over, it's all work."

Frowning, I lock eyes with her. "I'll probably regret asking this," I pause to think whether I shouldn't just keep quiet, but then push through, "Why do you bother with me then?"

She lets out another chuckle. "Damn, you can't even say it, can you?" Then she fucking mimics *Donkey*, "You're so wrapped up in layers, onion boy, you're afraid of your own feelings." Leaning back against the chair, she glances away from me and out the window, and then she murmurs, "You're worth the work."

Her words make my heart constrict, and then there's a burst of warmth in my chest. Frowning, I focus on the new emotion.

Is it gratitude? Maybe it's because I'm flattered?

CARLA

When I glance back at Noah, he's deep in thought, as if he's busy working out some impossible equation.

I place my hand on his thigh, and it instantly snaps him out of his thoughts. Leaning toward him, I say, "Relax, Noah. You're going to burst a vein with all that thinking."

I get up and go to the kitchen, so I can refill my glass. As I take a sip, Jase comes into the kitchen. When his eyes land on me, he comes to throw his arm around my shoulders, giving me a sideways hug. "How's school?" He takes the glass from my hands and takes a sip before handing it back.

I shrug. "It's okay."

"And the workload?" He asks as he helps himself to a slice of pizza.

"A lot. I've spent most of my time in the library."

"You'll get into the swing of things," he says. My brother's eyes lock on me, and then he tilts his head. "Besides school, is everything else okay? No one's giving you shit?"

Jase is the most perceptive person I know. I shrug again. "It's different from high school. You know? It's... lonely."

He takes a step closer to me, concern tightening his features. "What do you mean it's lonely? You have the other girls. Forest and Aria are also there."

"Yeah," I smile at him so he won't worry. "I'm just struggling to adjust. Don't mind me."

Jase's eyes sharpen on my face, then he asks, "There's nothing else bothering you?"

I shake my head, and stepping forward, I wrap my arms around his waist and rest my cheek against his shoulder. "I'm good, but you know what would help a lot?"

Jase hugs me back, muttering, "What?"

"All your notes and assignments." I pull back, and grinning at him, I say, "Pretty please, Jase."

"On one condition." A sneaky grin tugs at his lips. "Admit I'm the smarter one."

I scrunch my nose and pull a disgruntled face, then mutter, "You're smarter."

A victorious smile splits over his face. "I'll email them tomorrow."

"Thanks." I watch as he walks out, then I whisper, "I didn't say you're smarter than me, though." Letting out a chuckle, I take a sip from my wine.

Walking back into the living room, Jase has taken Mila's seat, and he has her on his lap, then he says, "Remind me to email all my notes from my MBA to Carla."

Mila glances at me. "Are you struggling with the work? I can help."

I sit back down next to Noah. "I'll be okay. Thanks, though."

Noah looks down at me. "It's only been a week. What could you possibly be struggling with?"

I slant my eyes up at him. "And here I thought we were doing so well."

He frowns. "I'm asking so I'll know what you need help with."

My eyebrows dart up. "Wow, you suck at offering help." Then I give him the sweetest smile I can conjure up. "But it's so heartwarming to know you *care*. I'm good, though."

Noah tilts his head at me. "You're not going to stop with the caring shit, are you?"

I shake my head and impersonate him, "Nope." I lock eyes with him. "Not until you admit you don't hate me."

A shocked expression flashes over his way-too-hot features. "I don't hate you." Then he frowns again. "You think I hate you?"

I shrug and take a sip from my glass before muttering, "With the intensity of a thousand suns." Lowering my voice, so only Noah will hear, I mutter, "You tell a guy you love him, and all of a sudden, you're public enemy number one."

Noah leans closer as well, whispering, "I just wanted to give you space so you could… you know… move on."

Turning my head, our eyes connect, and there's instantly an explosive current jumping between us.

Unable to stop myself, I ask, "Am I really the only one who feels this?"

"Feels what?" Noah pulls back, and bringing his hand to his face, he rests his chin on his thumb. I watch as his mind begins to work overtime again, trying to figure something out.

As brilliant as this man is, he can be slow when it comes to the emotional side of things.

I pat his thigh again. "Don't overthink things. I wasn't expecting an answer."

Chapter 6

NOAH

Sitting in our suite's living room, I read a study done by Havard Medical School. It's on love and the effects it has on the brain.

Levels of the stress hormone cortisol increase during the initial phase of romantic love, marshaling our bodies to cope with the "crisis" at hand.

"Well, that fucking explains it," I mutter. "Carla's definitely a crisis at hand."

I keep reading, and it just says what I already knew. It's just a chemical reaction.

Carla comes into the suite, a frown on her forehead. When she sees me, she drops down right next to me and says, "You will not believe who I just ran into."

I quickly lock my phone and set it aside. "Who?"

"Kennedy Quinn." Her gaze turns to me, and I can see the worry darkening her eyes. "Forest's ex-girlfriend."

Not following, I ask, "Yeah? Why are you worried?"

"Because Forest and Aria are 'dating'."

Still not understanding, I ask, "Why would that be a problem?"

Carla turns her body toward mine, and she rests her knee against my thigh. My eyes dart down as oxytocin, dopamine, and serotonin starts to flood my brain.

Nothing but chemicals, Noah. You're fine.

"It's supposed to be a fake relationship, remember. If they took things to the next level, Aria's not going to take Kennedy's return well."

"Oh… right." I'm too fucking focused on the emotions spreading through me to pay much attention to what Carla's saying.

"I'm sure they'll be okay," she murmurs, not sounding too convinced.

My gaze lifts to Carla's face as she worries about Forest and Aria, and I take in her features. Her chocolate-colored irises, her high cheekbones, and full lips that smile so easily. My eyes lower to her neck, her silky-looking skin, and down to her collarbones. When my sight focuses on the cleavage peeking from her shirt, my heartbeat starts to speed up.

"Do I have something on my shirt?" Carla glances down, and it has me shooting up from the couch.

"Nope. Nice… ah… shirt." Feeling frazzled, I dart down the hallway to my room.

Come Monday, I'm no closer to understanding these sudden and totally unwelcome feelings I have whenever Carla is near me.

It makes me feel off-balance and moody.

Coming out of the classroom, I'm also bored out of my mind. I'm only here to get the degree, but damn, the work isn't challenging at all.

Taking my phone out of my pocket, I text my mother.

N: Tell me something interesting.

I keep my phone in my hand so I'll feel when it vibrates. Walking out of the building, I head toward the dorms.

"Hey, roomie," Carla calls from behind me.

I glance over my shoulder and see that she's jogging toward me. My gaze drops to her breasts as they bounce, and I instantly feel confounded again.

Carla catches up to me and wrapping her arm around my back, she gives me a sideways hug. "Aren't you going for lunch?"

"Nope."

She glances up at me. "Is the cease-fire over?"

I shake my head.

"Bad mood?"

I shake my head again.

"Wow, aren't you talkative today," she quips.

Walking faster, I mutter, "You're talkative enough for the both of us."

As Carla walks away from me, she mutters, "Grumpy."

My phone buzzes, and I quickly open the text from Mom.

M: Hey, my boy. Just hold out. You're almost done with your studies. In the meanwhile, here you go… I have a twenty-year-old male patient who was rushed in with an aneurysm. Basically, the thoracic aorta consists of the aortic root…

I keep reading as I head into the dorm and up to the suite. Every word makes me feel less restless until I'm back to feeling in control of my emotions.

I shove thoughts of Carla way down, even though I know I won't be able to avoid them forever.

CARLA

I walk into the restaurant and see Forest and Aria already sitting at our table. As I take a seat, I almost make a comment about them being caught in their own little bubble, but instead impersonate *Scar* from the *Lion King*, "I'm surrounded by idiots."

Aria chuckles. "What happened?"

I haven't told them about Noah's weird behavior, so I just mutter, "Noah."

Movement behind Forest catches my attention, and when I see Kennedy, my eyes widen.

Shit, here we go.

Forest is clearly startled by the sight of her, and Aria looks like she's going to be sick. At least I gave her a heads up this morning that I ran into Kennedy last night.

Kennedy's all smiles as she asks, "Tell me everything I've missed out on."

Hoping Forest and Aria will come forward with the fact that they're more than friends, I lean over to Kennedy and say, "Prepare yourself for this. Forest and Aria are in a fake relationship."

My gaze is sharp on my two friends to catch their reaction. Forest instantly looks unhappy, and Aria shrinks back against her chair.

Mhhh… just friends? Right?

Kennedy lets out a burst of laughter. "Yeah? Why?"

It's up to me to explain, "Forest didn't date after you left, and rumors started going around that there's something wrong with him."

Kennedy's eyes widen, and she turns to Forest. "Oh my gosh! Really?"

He just nods, letting out an uncomfortable chuckle.

When Forest and Aria decided on having this fake relationship, I drew up a contract so I wouldn't be caught in the middle if it backfired. Never did I think they'd forego one of the cardinal rules and actually start dating. The fact that they haven't bothered to tell me hurts like a bitch, and it makes me wonder just how much I mean to them.

My attention is drawn back to the conversation when Aria gets up, mumbling, "I have to get to class. We should catch up later."

When Forest gets up to go after her, there's zero doubt left in my mind. They're dating for real.

I order my lunch and focus on catching up with Kennedy because she's not a bad person at all. We all pretty much got along with her when she dated Forest. While she tells me about her experiences while living abroad, my thoughts keep whirling around Forest and Aria.

We've been best friends since I can remember, and for the first time, I'm not part of the group anymore. It sucks... and causes my heart to ache.

I finish my meal, and getting up, I smile at Kennedy, "Catch you later."

Walking out of the restaurant, I've never felt more out of place and lonely than I do at this moment.

I head back to the suite to be alone with my misery, but when I walk in, Noah's in front of the TV, watching *CNN* news.

I sit down next to him and stare blankly at the TV screen. A couple of seconds pass, then I lean my head against his shoulder, whispering, "Just a couple of minutes, and I'll leave you alone."

He sits frozen for a bit, then asks, "Is everything okay?"

I shake my head. "I feel lonely."

Noah surprises me by lifting his arm and wrapping it around my shoulders. He pulls me into his side.

Not letting this opportunity pass me by, I snuggle against him and wrap my arm around his waist. "Thank you."

I take a deep breath of his scent and focus on the feel of his body against mine. My fingers grip his shirt as a sharp ache shoots through my heart.

God, I want more of this.

My body shudders from how amazing it feels to be held by Noah.

He tightens his arm around me, and lifting his other hand, he presses it against the side of my head, and then I feel his breath stir over the top of my head.

I freeze, and all my senses are focused on Noah as he presses a kiss to my hair. I forget to breathe, and my heart could've stopped, and I wouldn't have noticed.

I'm filled with the love I've never gotten to express, and it makes my eyes tear up.

I love you so much. Please love me back.

Noah continues to watch the news, and I keep still, so he won't get annoyed from having to hold me. My eyes begin to grow heavy, and then I'm unable to keep them open.

Chapter 7

NOAH

When Carla's body relaxes against mine, I glance down, and seeing she's asleep, I let out a deep breath.

I stare at her while emotions war inside of me, everything from tenderness to apprehension.

Her head slides down my chest, and before she can faceplant against my cock, I slip my hand under her cheek and position her on my thigh.

Slowly, I pull my hand from under her, but the movement still makes her stir. She rubs her cheek against my thigh before curling into a little ball.

Staring at Carla, I lift my hand to her forehead and carefully brush her brown curls away from her face.

My gaze drifts to where my arm is resting on her side. I move my left hand until my fingers lightly brush over her arm.

Her skin is soft.

With my right hand, I pinch a curl between my pointer finger and thumb.

Also soft.

Since the night she told me she loves me and I watched her run up the stairs, I haven't seen Carla vulnerable until today. It makes a weird protective feeling flutter to life.

Another new emotion to try and process.

The news on the TV is totally forgotten as I take in the girl sleeping on my lap.

Girl?

Is she really still a girl?

I take in her curves and the cleavage, which is more prominent now that's she's lying on her side.

No, Carla's definitely not a little girl.

Carla's grown up, and now that she's a woman, I'm not so sure the age difference matters anymore.

Maybe I should give a relationship with her a try? She knows what I'm like… that I'm different. Still, she hasn't given up on me, and it's been years. That has to count for something.

My eyes lock on Carla's face, and I allow myself to experience the emotions she brings out in me. My heart begins to beat faster, and my lips part as my breathing speeds up.

Whether it's a chemical reaction or more, Carla makes me feel things I've never felt before. Interest, desire, protectiveness, the need to dominate her.

There's a need to get to know every single thing about her until she's no longer a mystery.

But I've hurt her once before, and I really don't want to cause her any further heartache. What if it turns out I can't be with her? That would break her heart again. Just because she loves me, it doesn't give me the right to use her as if she's some experiment.

Carla deserves a man who will worship the ground she walks on. She deserves better than a man who struggles to deal with emotions.

The thought of Carla dating another man makes my jaw clench and my breathing speed up. I feel a possessive twinge and the urge to punch something.

Tilting my head, I try to process the new emotions.

Fuck, Carla is like an out of control rollercoaster, and I'm not sure I'll survive the ride.

Needing to examine the mess in my head and chest, I carefully slip my arms under Carla and getting up, I carry her to her bedroom. I set her down on her bed, and in a moment of insanity, I lean over her and press my mouth to her temple.

My eyes drift shut as I take in the feel of her skin against my lips. Pulling back, I rush out of her room and head to my own.

Opening my phone, I dial Dash's number. I need to speak to someone who will give me some answers, and my sister is the only person I can think of. She takes after my father, where I'm more like my mother, but Dash understands how my mind works.

"Hi, Noah," her voice comes over the line. "How are you?"

"Hey, I'm okay," I rub tiredly over my forehead. "Can I ask you something?"

"Sure." I hear her move around and a door shutting.

"What is… how…" I struggle to find the right words. "So, there's this girl…"

Dash lets out a chuckle. "And you're confused about how you feel?"

My sister always gets me.

"Yeah." I let out a sigh.

"Okay, let me try and explain it in a way you'll understand. Give me a minute to think." I listen to my sister's breathing, then she says, "Love is like a driven force. It comes from the part in your mind that craves things, like chocolate, a hug, or getting an A on a test. As humans, we're driven to procreate, and when you see a suitable mate, you feel attraction toward them. You crave the person, so to speak." She pauses then asks, "Am I making sense?"

"Yeah... but," I suck in a deep breath, then say, "the girl is Carla Reyes."

"Oh, she's stunning. Of course, you'd feel attracted to her. You move in the same circle. She comes from a similar background as you. She's a suitable mate for you, and you recognize that."

"I'm glad you think so," I mutter.

"Stop overthinking things and enjoy the process, Noah."

Easier said than done.

I talk with my sister for a little while longer before hanging up.

Sitting down on the edge of my bed, I let out a sigh.

Should I just go for it and see if things can work between Carla and me?

No, I should wait.

Yeah, I'll wait and see if these emotions keep growing.

CARLA

Walking back to the suite after I overheard Forest tell Kennedy that he's in a relationship with Aria, hurt squeezes at my heart.

So much for us being related. Were they even going to tell me?

Before coming to Trinity Academy and signing the stupid fake relationship contract, which doesn't mean shit, we were so close. Now it feels like I'm nothing to them.

I walk to my room and grab the contract we signed. Taking the piece of paper from my drawer, I head to the living room. I lean back against the couch as my mind races to find an excuse why Forest and Aria would just cut me off like that.

Tonight I want answers. I'm done being cast aside.

I don't have to wait long before Aria walks into the suite.

"The relationship is real?" I ask as I try to swallow back the heartache. "So much for us being best friends. Right?"

Before she can answer me, Forest comes in behind her.

My gaze snaps to my cousin. "You lied to me."

"I didn't lie to you," Forest practically growls at me. "While we're slinging accusations at each other, where the hell do you get off telling Kennedy that Aria and I are in a fake relationship? You had no right to do that."

Feeling disappointed, I move closer to Forest. "If the two of you hadn't kept it from me, I would've known to keep my mouth shut. Don't you dare turn this on me." I dart back to the couch and grab the contract. Tearing it in half, I try to keep from crying as I say, "This show is over. You both crossed the line and then kept it from me. What am I to the two of you? Chopped liver?" I take a deep breath of air, but it doesn't help to lessen the pain.

"I'm sorry, Carla," Aria says. "I didn't want to drag you into it."

That's all she has to say? They've ignored me for two weeks, and that's all I get?

Anger begins to whirl with the loneliness I've felt because they just left me. "You both dragged me into this mess the day you decided this fake relationship was the answer to all your problems. I didn't have much choice in the matter." I suck in a breath of air as I struggle not to cry, and then I admit how they made me feel, "You've been living in your little bubble since school started. I'm not even a part of the group anymore. It hurts finding out just

74

how little you mean to the two people who were supposed to be your best friends."

Knowing I'm about to burst into tears any second, I shake my head and turn away from them. As the first tear falls, I slam into a wall of muscle. Instinctively I know it's Noah, and when his arms wrap around me, it becomes near impossible to not just break down and sob my heart out against his chest.

Who would've thought Noah would become the only person I have left to turn to?

"You both need to sort out your shit," Noah snaps at them.

"It was all an act, Carla. One of us just forgot. Don't worry, there's no relationship," Aria suddenly says.

Seriously, now she's going to lie to me as well?

Pulling away from Noah, I turn to face her. "It didn't look like that."

"I know. I'm sorry. I lost control," Aria explains while Forest looks like he's taken a punch to the gut. "Call it temporary insanity. I'm sorry I hurt you. I love you and don't want this to come between us. Can… can't we forget this happened? I'll do anything to fix things."

Before I can reply, Noah takes hold of my hand and glaring at Forest and Aria, he says, "Sort this shit out now.

It's affecting everyone." He pulls me down the hallway, and I'm a little too stunned to react. "Let's give them some privacy," he mutters before he drags me into my room and slams the door shut behind us.

When Noah frames my face with his hands, and he wipes the tears from my cheeks with his thumbs, I can only stare at him.

What the hell is going on?

He must take my stunned silence for something else because he wraps his arms around me and pulling me tightly against this chest, he asks, "Is that why you said you felt lonely?"

His question yanks me out of the stupor, and it makes the heartache rise back to the surface. Nodding against his chest, I feel overwhelmed by the kindness he's showing me and from the fight I just had with Aria and Forest.

Forest didn't even bother saying anything.

The thought makes a sob flutter over my lips, and I'm unable to keep the tears back any longer.

Noah tightens his hold on me, and pressing a kiss to the side of my head, he murmurs, "It's okay. Shh… it's okay. I might be an ass most of the time, but I'm here."

His words only make the tears fall faster. It brings the realization that I'm not just crying about what happened with Forest and Aria, but also because of Noah.

All the tension of being around him and loving him but not having my feelings returned is starting to wear me thin. I want to push him away and tell him I'm going to stop loving him, but I can't. Instead, I press closer to him, needing him more than my next breath.

I'll never be able to stop loving this man, and it's the loneliest feeling ever.

Chapter 8

NOAH

Carla crying against my chest is pure torture. Wanting to make her feel better, I press a kiss to the side of her head, but it only makes her cry harder.

Feeling panicky, I hold her tighter. "Shh… it's okay."

God, how do I calm her down?

I try rubbing a hand over her back, but when that doesn't work, the panic grows inside of me until I pull back, and framing her face, I press my mouth to hers.

Seconds later, shock at what I'm doing makes me yank back. I stare at her equally stunned expression. But then I realize she stopped crying, and a smile splits over my face. "Hey, it worked. You stopped crying."

The surprised expression on her face is quickly replaced with a frown. "You kissed me because I was crying?"

I shrug. "It worked, though."

She gasps for air, and then she sputters, "You freaking kissed me to make me stop crying? Seriously?"

I shrug again. "It's no big deal. It calmed you down…" Looking at the frown on her face, I add, "Kind of."

Carla stares at me, and then she shakes her head. "You can't just lay a kiss on me like that. I wasn't prepared. I didn't take any of it in. That's unfair, Noah."

I begin to frown. "It's unfair?"

"Yeah. The one time you kiss me, and I'm a hot mess." She shakes her head again. "Hell no. I want a do-over."

"Do-over?" I ask like an idiot.

Carla closes the distance between us, and wrapping her fingers around the back of my neck, she pulls me down while pushing herself up on her toes. Her mouth presses against mine, and then it feels like my IQ drops to zero, and my hormones take over.

Carla's lips move, and the touch is tentative as if she's asking permission. While one of my hands go to her back, the other slips into her hair so I can hold her to me. My lips part, and the moment my tongue slips inside the warmth of her mouth, she lets out a throaty sound of pleasure, which makes me harden instantly.

I lose total control to my dominant side, and gripping her tighter, my tongue brushes hard strokes against hers. Carla's taste… the feel of her body… the sensuality pouring off of her – it's all intoxicating. My heart thunders against my ribs as emotions explode through me like fireworks. My skin sizzles to life, begging for her touch. The electric current that's been humming between us grows a thousand times stronger in voltage, threatening to electrocute us.

I have no idea for how long I devour her mouth, and when she pulls back, I'm dead sure I wouldn't have stopped if it was up to me.

Carla stares at me, breathless and wide-eyed.

I catch my breath and lifting a hand, I wipe over my face as I move back so I can sit on her bed. I feel out of my depth and don't know where to begin or how to address the elephant in the room.

Carla comes to sit down next to me, and for a long moment, we both just stare ahead of us.

She clears her throat and adjusts her pink long sleeve shirt that's dropped from her shoulder. "So... that just happened."

"Yeah," I murmur. I try to search for the right words to say, but seeing as I suck at communicating with the opposite sex, I'm left speechless.

Carla turns her body toward mine and reaches for my hand. "Do you need time to process the kiss?"

Surprised, my eyes dart to hers. "We don't have to talk about it right now?"

The corner of her mouth lifts as she shakes her head. "I know you, Noah. You need time to figure out what it means. I can wait."

"You're not angry?" I ask because any other girl would probably tell me to go to hell.

"Not at all." A beautiful smile spreads over her face. "You kissed me." She shrugs, and it makes the shirt slip down her shoulder again.

Pulling my hand free from hers, I tug the fabric back over her skin. "Technically, you kissed me."

Carla lets out a chuckle, "Yeah, but you're the one who took it further." Then she mimics *Sid* from *Ice Age*, "For a second there, I actually thought you were gonna eat me."

Chuckling, a smile forms around my lips, and for a moment, I just stare at her. I take in the happy glow on her face, and it makes warmth spread through my chest.

I'm responsible for that look on her face.

I wrap my hand around the back of her neck and pull her to me. Hugging her, I murmur, "You're turning out to be quite the surprise, Carla Reyes."

"Yeah?" she whispers as her arms circle my neck. "In a good way?"

I nod and squeeze her tighter to me. "I just need time. Okay?"

Again, Carla is the first to pull back. Her gaze locks with mine and seeing the love she feels for me almost makes me kiss her again. Instead, I get up and shove a hand in my pocket. I rub over the back of my neck with my other hand.

"It's okay, Noah," Carla says as she rises to her feet. "Go think. I'm fine."

I still hesitate, and unable to just leave, I lift my hand to her cheek. I lean down and press a kiss to her forehead. Before I pull back, I whisper, "Thank you for understanding me."

I let go of her and walk out of her room.

As soon as I shut my door behind me, I stand and stare at the carpet like a stupefied idiot.

It's clear Carla isn't a kid anymore, and seeing as that was the only reason I was keeping my distance from her, what's stopping me now?

Nothing.

Absolutely nothing.

CARLA

I fall back on my bed, and with the broadest grin, I stare up at the ceiling.

Holy. Shit.

That just happened.

Noah kissed me.

There was tongue.

Lots of tongue.

"Ahhhh….." I let out a happy shriek as I wiggle and shake my body on the mattress.

Suddenly my door opens, and I shoot up into a sitting position. Surprise ripples through me as Noah walks back into my room. He comes to take a seat again, and then he stares at the floor.

I sit absolutely still, not sure what this means. He couldn't possibly have thought about it already, could he?

After a couple of minutes, he lifts his head and turns to look at me. "I like you, Carla."

Oh, God. This is where he rejects me again.

My heart begins to shrivel into a tiny lump.

Then he murmurs, "I need to take things slow."

Huh?

I can only sit and blink at him.

He takes a deep breath, and a slight frown forms between his eyes. "I'm not good with emotions."

I nod, unable to form words.

"And I don't want to hurt you again."

I nod again, fisting my hands on my lap.

Noah notices and reaching for one of my hands, he wraps his strong fingers around mine.

"I want to try." His eyes stare into mine with the intensity of a nuclear bomb. I suck in a trembling breath as his words start to get through to me. "But, we need to take it slow. I need to adjust... to everything."

I nod like a freaking bobblehead.

Noah stares at me, then he says, "Now's a good time to say something."

"Oh," the word pops from me. I want to throw my arms around his neck and kiss him until we're both seconds away from dying due to oxygen-deprivation. I want to jump up and dance around the room while yelling at the top of my lungs with joy. I want to crumble into a ball and cry with relief. Instead, I whisper, "I'm good with everything you said."

Noah tilts his head and narrows his eyes on me. "Let it out before you explode."

As if my body was waiting for permission, I shoot forward and wrap my arms tightly around his neck. I bury my face against his warm skin and suck in a shaky breath as an overwhelming feeling shudders through me.

Finally. After all these years.

After not giving up and endlessly hoping, after all the tears, all the longing, all the dreaming about a future that might never be mine – Noah is willing to try.

"Thank you," I whisper, my voice hoarse from the happiness bursting through me like a million sunrays.

Noah wraps his arms around me, and he presses a kiss to my shoulder. "I need to say something."

I nod against him.

"When you told me you loved me, I'm sorry I broke your heart. I still stand by what I did, though. You were too young."

I pull back as I impersonate *Sid* again, "Ah, you know me, I'm too lazy to hold a grudge."

Noah lets out a chuckle.

Clearing my throat, I lift my eyes to his and ask, "But you're okay with us trying, right?"

The corner of his mouth lifts. "Yeah. You being eighteen changed things."

I scrunch my nose at him. "Is that the only reason?"

He shakes his head. "Nope."

A grin forms around my mouth, and when he keeps quiet, I jump on the bed. "Come on, you're killing me here."

He lets out a chuckle. "I've started developing feelings for you."

"Like?" the word rushes from me.

"Like… you'll have to wait while I try and figure out what they are," he teases me.

"Butterflies?" I ask.

Noah's grin grows, and he nods.

I wag my eyebrows. "Tingles down south?"

"Fuck." He lets out a bark of laughter. "You're not going to stop, are you?"

I shake my head but then concede anyway, not wanting to push him too hard. "I'm just teasing you."

We stare at each other for a moment, and it makes another burst of happiness rush through me.

"Can I ask you a question?" Noah asks, tilting his head.

"Sure."

"Why did you say I'm worth the work? What makes me worth it?"

I reach for his hand, and when I link my fingers with his, and I feel the familiar rush coursing through my veins,

I smile up at him. "Physically, you tick all of my boxes. You have a brilliant mind, and yeah, most people might not understand you, but to me, it's one hell of a turn-on," I answer directly. "Also, there's just something about you… almost edgy…" I take a deep breath. "It's addictive."

Noah's eyes are glued to mine as he asks, "You don't think I'm weird?"

Shaking my head, I murmur, "Everything but weird."

Noah nods, and when his gaze drifts to our joined hands, I know he's processing what I just said. After a minute, he brings his eyes back to mine. "You're good with slow, right?"

"Yes." I nod quickly.

"Let's see what happens, and then we can talk about… you know… taking things further," he says, clearly uncomfortable when it comes to thinking that far ahead.

I lean forward and press a kiss to his cheek. Pulling back, I murmur, "Let's give it a couple of weeks, and if you feel like you can't be in a relationship with me, then we can stick to being friends. I just want you to know I'm thankful that you're trying, at least."

Noah looks at me like I'm an unsolved mystery, then he climbs to his feet. "I'm going to head to bed."

"Okay." I smile at him as I get up. "Sweet dreams."

He leans forward and presses a tender kiss to my forehead. "Night."

I watch him leave and then do a happy dance before falling back on my bed.

Chapter 9

CARLA

I wake up, and my first thought is of Noah. A wide smile stretches over my face as I get up to prepare for the day.

Okay, Carla. You need to act all cool around him. Give him the time he needs. At least you've leveled up to friendship status.

I'm so freaking happy it feels like I'm bursting at the seams. I take a cute dress from my closet and my favorite pair of boots. When I'm dressed, and I've done my make-up, I grab my three-quarter sleeve jacket and shrug it on.

Walking out of my room, my eyes instantly go to Noah's door, and seeing it's closed, I head down the hallway.

I find Hana in the kitchen, already sipping on her coffee. "Morning." I grin at her as I pour myself a cup.

"Morning." Hana's gaze sharpens on me. "You look happy. What happened?"

I shrug. "I just slept like a rock."

"Uh-huh," she mumbles, clearly not believing me.

I lean back against the counter and say, "Noah and I made peace."

Her eyebrows pop up. "That is good news. I'm glad to hear things are better between the two of you."

Forest comes into the kitchen, and before I can say anything, he hugs me, murmuring, "I'm sorry you got caught in the shitstorm."

Pulling back, I reply, "I was just shocked last night. Sorry for the dramatics." I lock eyes with my cousin and search for any sign that he's not okay, then I ask, "How are you holding up?"

He gets himself a cup of coffee. "I'll be okay."

Hana gives him the same look she gave me a minute ago. "Yeah?"

Forest nods, focusing on preparing the coffee.

"I talked with Aria," Hana mentions.

"How did that go?" he asks.

"You're both hurting," Hana answers him. "Why can't you just sit down and talk like adults?"

He sucks in a deep breath. "I tried." Shaking his head, he sounds tired when he murmurs, "Trust me, I tried. She won't open up to me."

Placing my hand on his shoulder, I say, "Aria's scared."

He nods. "I know. I don't know how to reassure her. I've tried everything."

"You show her she has nothing to be afraid of," Hana says. "Just be there for her. Once she sees you're not going anywhere, I'm sure she'll come around."

"That was the plan," he replies. Finishing his coffee, he rinses the cup, then says, "I'll catch you later."

The second he leaves, I look back to Hana and ask, "They'll be okay, right?"

Hana nods. "Yeah. If Jade and Hunter can work through their problems, Aria and Forest will be fine." Hana grabs her bag, then says, "I'll see you later. Have a good day."

"You too." While drinking my coffee, my happiness is dimmed by what's happening with Forest and Aria.

I need to talk to Aria.

Last night I hashed things out with Aria, and I feel much better now that the mess has been cleared up between myself and my friends.

I can see things are tense between the two of them, but I know I can't get involved. It's up to them to decide whether they want to be in a relationship or not.

After I'm done with my classes, I spend my entire afternoon in the library. I didn't expect the workload to be so overwhelming, but I'll be damned if I buckle under the pressure. If Jase could do it, so can I.

Leaving the library, my phone begins to ring. Seeing Mom's name flashing on the screen, I smile as I answer, "Hi, Mom."

"Hi, sweetie, how's school?" I can hear pots and utensils clanking in the background.

"School is good. Just a lot of work. Are you busy preparing dinner?"

Damn, I miss Mom's cooking.

"Yeah. Your father wants chicken piccata with lemon sauce and those cheese and herb potato fans you love so much."

Instantly my mouth begins to water, and I change direction to where my car is parked. "Mind if I come over?"

Mom lets out a chuckle. "That's a stupid question."

My smile widens. "I'll be there in ten minutes."

I hang up and tuck my phone into my bag. Reaching the vehicle, I slide behind the steering wheel and steer the car off the campus.

When I park in the driveway, I leave my bag, seeing as I won't need it, and hurry to the front door. Using my set of keys, I let myself in and make my way to the spacious kitchen.

"Hey," I say as I walk to where Mom is busy preparing the meal. I press a kiss to her cheek.

"If I knew all it would take to get you to visit was making potato fans, I would've done it the first day you moved out," Mom teases while I quickly wash my hands.

I let out a chuckle as I dry off the excess water. I take my place next to Mom, and grabbing a potato half, I begin slicing strips into it.

"Sooo…" Mom draws the word out, "what's new? How does it feel to live in the dorm? Have you made any new friends?"

I keep my gaze on the potato, so I don't cut my fingers off as I answer, "I didn't expect it to be such a huge adjustment, but I'm getting the hang of things now. At first, it felt like I was thrown into an alternate universe."

"Yeah, it can be daunting," Mom agrees. "When I started at Trinity, I only knew Layla and Kingsley, and we weren't close yet."

"That must've been hard." I glance at Mom. "How did you cope?"

She gives me a warm smile. "I just powered through it, and after a while, I got used to how things worked." There's a moment's silence, then she asks, "Any guys caught your eye yet?"

I let out a sputter of laughter. Mom knows I've been in love with Noah for years because there's nothing I hide from her. "Nah, it's still only Noah."

"And? How is it living in the same suite as him?" Her hands still as her eyes focus on me.

I shrug. "We're actually trying to be friends. It's a relief."

"That's good to hear," Mom murmurs.

Then the corner of my mouth lifts and pausing with the work for a moment, I murmur, "We kissed."

"Oh my God," Mom shrieks, and then she's yanking me into a hug and bouncing with me. "I'm so happy for you!" Mom pulls back and gives me a big smile. "And... how was it?"

I begin to laugh as my cheeks flush. "So much better than I thought it would be." I let out a sigh. "He was... I was..." I sigh. "It was perfect."

Mom cups my cheeks with her hand. "Aww... I'm glad."

"He said he needs time to process everything." I begin to slice the potatoes again. "So I'm giving him space. I'm just glad he's willing to try."

"Me too," Mom murmurs. "I know how much you love him, and I just want you to be happy."

A soft smile plays around my lips as I say, "I am. I really am."

NOAH

When three days have passed, I'm surprised Carla hasn't come to talk to me yet. Whenever I run into her, she just smiles as if nothing happened between us.

I'm beginning to realize there's much more to Carla than meets the eye. She's probably one of the most patient people I know. Any other girl would've told me to get lost by now.

Carla is probably going to San Francisco with Forest and Aria for Aria's art exhibition. The thought of Carla not being here this weekend gets to me, though.

I'll talk to her once she gets back. After this past week and realizing how well she understands me, I'm ready to take the next step.

Also, I want to see if the physical side of things will work between us.

After that kiss, do you seriously have any doubts?
Nope.

When I walk down the hallway, I hear Carla say, "Can you go to the drug store and get me some flu meds?"

She's sick?

"Do you feel sick?" I hear Forest ask.

"Yeah. My body aches all over, and my throat feels like someone shoved thorns down it."

I walk into the living room, and the instant I see her feverish face, I go to take her hand while telling Forest, "I'll make sure she gets meds in her."

"He's going to drug and kill me," Carla groans, but I can hear the playful tone in her voice.

"Don't give me any ideas," I tease her as I drag her back to her room. "Climb back in bed."

Without any argument, she lies down and snuggles into her pillow, then she asks, "Are we going to play doctor-patient?"

I tilt my head at her. "No, you're going to rest and get better." My eyes scan over her face, and then I place the back of my hand against her forehead. Feeling the heat coming off her, I say, "I'll get you flu medicine and chicken soup."

"I will not eat chicken soup. Don't you dare order it," she grumbles at me.

"Chicken soup?" Aria asks as she comes into the room.

"Yeah, she's sick," I mutter. Slanting my eyes at Carla, I add, "And a terrible patient."

"Aww... no. So you can't come tonight?" Aria asks as she goes to feel Carla's forehead. "Do you have meds? Should I go get you some?"

"I've got it covered," I say. "Don't worry about her."

"Worry about me," Carla groans. "I'm stuck with the tin man."

When my gaze darts to her, she winks at me.

Aria lets out a chuckle as she says, "Damn, we'll miss you."

I feel a sudden burst of relief and happiness that Carla's staying home, and do my best to not let it show on my face.

"You go kick ass," Carla grins as she turns onto her side. "I'm just going to sleep it off."

"I'll call later to check on you," Aria says.

"Enjoy the night, guys."

When Forest and Aria leaves, I turn back to Carla. "Tin man?"

"Yeah, but you're a hot tin man." She begins to chuckle, but it turns into a cough.

I sit down next to her and rub a hand over her back. "I'm going to run to the store quickly. Try to get some sleep. Okay?"

Carla nods, then she murmurs, "Thank you."

Leaning over her, I press a kiss to her feverish forehead, and then I rush out of the suite.

After getting everything Carla will need to get better, I unpack the bags on the kitchen island. I place the juices in the fridge and taking a bottle of water and the medicine, I head back to her room.

She's kicked off the covers and lying on her side, it looks like she's asleep. She's wearing cotton shorts and a tight t-shirt, which make her body look hot as fuck.

Pushing the desire to the side, I set the meds down on her bedside table. The sound makes Carla turn onto her back.

"Sit up," I murmur as I take a seat on the side of the bed. I hold the water out to her and then begin to go through all the medicine. When she's taken everything, and her eyes drift closed, I say, "Lie down again and get some sleep."

She does as I say, and then she asks, "Can you turn up the AC? It's hot."

"The ibuprofen will help with the fever." I get up and go get a bowl of ice. Walking back into her room, I go to her ensuite bathroom to grab a cloth. Pouring water over the ice, I soak the cloth until it's cool. I squeeze out the excess water then begin to slowly wipe down her arms. I keep rinsing the cloth, and as I move down to her legs, she lets out a moan.

"So good," she murmurs.

My hands itch to touch her, but I keep wiping over her heated skin before placing the cool cloth over her forehead.

Carla's eyes drift closed again as she whispers, "Thank you."

My lips curve up. "You're welcome."

I sit and watch as she falls asleep. Then I pull my phone from my pocket and begin to read an article about NASA awarding a contract to a university to provide freezers for science samples aboard the International Space Station.

Every couple of minutes, my gaze drifts over Carla, and eventually, I turn off the device and just stare at her.

I reach for her thigh and brush my knuckles over her skin. A current instantly zaps between us, and fascinated by how she makes me feel, I brush my fingers up to the edge of her shorts.

Carla's eyes open, and I instantly regret waking her. "Sorry."

She shakes her head. "I love that you're staying with me, but I don't want you to catch this cold, or flu, or whatever it is."

"I'll be fine," I set her mind at ease. "Can I get you something to eat?"

She shakes her head. "No, thanks. I'm not hungry."

"A juice? We have to keep you hydrated."

A smile tugs at her mouth. "Careful, I could get used to you taking care of me."

I give her hand a squeeze then rise to my feet so I can get her an orange juice.

Chapter 10

CARLA

Every time I wake up, it's to see Noah sitting next to me. He's reading something on his phone, and it gives me time to stare at him.

My gaze drifts over him. It's so easy to be deceived by his good looks, but he's like an onion. There are so many layers to him. From his hot as hell body to his mind that continually needs to be fed.

"If you have me, you want to share me," I murmur, making Noah's eyes instantly dart to me. "If you share me, you don't have me. What am I?"

A grin tugs at his mouth. "A secret."

I try to think of another riddle. "You're escaping a labyrinth, and there are three doors in front of you. The door to the left leads to a raging inferno. The one in the center leads to a deadly assassin. The other on the right leads to a lion that hasn't eaten in three months. Which door do you choose?"

He smiles and shakes his head. "The lion hasn't eaten in three months, so he's dead."

I scrunch my nose at him. "I'll have to up my game."

Noah places his hand against my forehead. "How do you feel?"

"Much better and hungry." When he gets up, I add, "I just want to shower, then I'd like to sit in the living room. I'm tired of the bed."

"Will you try to have chicken soup?" Noah asks. "It will help you feel better."

Not able to resist him, I mutter, "Fine."

I get a broad smile as a reward before he leaves my room. I notice it's already ten pm. Checking my phone, I see I have a text from Forest.

F: I hope you're feeling better. Aria won.

C: Whooo-Hooo! Tell her congrats from me. We'll celebrate when you get back. I'm feeling much better. Have fun while you're there. x

Forcing myself up, I go shower. When I'm dressed in comfy clothes, I tie my hair in a ponytail, and grabbing my pillow, I walk to the living room.

I find Noah in the kitchen, in front of a bowl of soup and a glass of orange juice. "Come eat."

I drop my pillow on one of the couches and then sit down on one of the stools situated around the island. "Thank you for taking care of me."

Noah comes to take a seat next to me with a cheeseburger and shoestring fries for himself. He waits until I eat a spoonful of the soup, and only then does he turn his attention to his own food.

"Forest texted me. Aria won the competition," I inform Noah before I scoop up another spoonful of soup.

"That's great news," he says, then he admits, "I haven't seen any of her work yet."

"She's really good. I have a photo of one of her pieces on my phone." I slide off the stool and go get the device from my room. Opening up my gallery, I search for the photo as I walk back to the kitchen. I turn the screen to Noah so he can see. "She painted this one for our senior year."

One of Noah's eyebrows raises slightly. "Damn, that's an amazing piece."

There's a proud smile on my face as I sit down again. "Yeah."

We continue with our meals, and the thought hits me that Noah has spent the entire day with me. It means everything to me. Still, I ask, "It's a Saturday night. Didn't you have any plans?"

He swallows the bite down, then wipes his mouth with a napkin before he replies, "Nothing I couldn't cancel."

His answer makes a grin spread over my face.

When we're done with our meals, I pick up my pillow and sit down on the couch. Noah grabs the TV remote and then comes to take a seat next to me.

Screw that.

I throw the pillow onto one of the other couches, and lifting his arm, I position it around my shoulders. Cuddling up against him, I murmur, "Mhh... you're better than a pillow."

He lets out a chuckle while turning on the TV, then he asks, "What do you want to watch?"

"Anything. I'll probably fall asleep halfway through."

"Are you okay with a documentary?"

My lips curve up. "Sure."

He goes to Netflix and puts on *Dancing with the Birds*. As he gets lost in the show, his fingers begin to brush up and down my arm, and the touch makes a kaleidoscope of butterflies take flight in my stomach.

Suddenly Noah murmurs, "I'm glad you didn't go with Forest and Aria."

I glance up at him. "Yeah?"

He nods, his eyes not leaving the TV screen. "I was thinking we could slowly start with a relationship."

I sit up, and turning my body toward him, I cross my legs in front of me. "Like... dating?" I ask to make sure.

My heart begins to beat faster as I wait for Noah's answer. He turns off the TV, and then his eyes lock on mine.

"Yes, dating," he answers, making a burst of happiness rush through my heart. "But I still want to take it slow."

I nod quickly. "I'm fine with taking things slow. No rush."

Noah reaches for my hand and when his fingers brush against mine, tingles race over my skin. My breaths begin to speed up as I stare deep into his eyes. He brings his other hand to the back of my head, and then he pulls me closer as he leans in. My breath stalls in my throat as the distance shrinks between us, and all my senses heighten, not wanting to miss a thing.

Noah's lips brush softly against mine, and then he pulls back an inch. I feel his breaths on my face, and it makes an intense sensation spread through my body. My abdomen tightens, and my heart begins to thunder in my chest. When his lips brush against mine again, it feels like my soul might burst from all the happiness I'm filled with.

He pulls back, and the corner of his mouth lifts as his eyes drift over my face.

NOAH

My phone begins to ring, disrupting the intimate moment between us. I dig the device out of my pocket and frown when I see Kao's name flashing on the screen. "Hey, what's up?"

"Hi, I don't know if you heard yet, but there was an earthquake in San Francisco. Forest and Aria are missing," Kao says.

My mind instantly begins to race, pulling up stats about earthquakes and survival rates.

"Shit," is all I manage to say, though.

Carla's phone starts to ring, and before I can grab hold of her hand to keep her from answering, she darts up and dashes to the kitchen, where she left the device.

Fuck, this is bad.

"Mr. Reyes is keeping us updated. They've taken a flight to San Francisco to arrange a search party with the Chargills'."

"That's good," I answer, for lack of finding the right words. "Keep us updated, please."

"Will do." Kao pauses, then he says, "Take care of Carla. She'll be worried and upset. Comfort her."

"Yeah, sure," I mutter.

The call ends, and I get up from the couch. Only then does the shock from the news hit, rippling through my body. My mind scrambles faster for every bit of information I have on earthquakes as I walk to where Carla stands.

Her face pales, and she freezes as if she's caught in a trance. Then her hand begins to tremble, and her breathing speeds up.

An icy shiver rushes over my body, causing weird prickles to spread over my skin.

A couple of seconds later, she murmurs, "Ah... No. Noah's here." Her gaze darts to mine as she says, "Love you too, Daddy. Bye."

Her hand drops limply to her side as I move in front of her. "Did your dad tell you about Forest and Aria?" I ask.

She nods slowly.

I tilt my head to catch her eyes, then I say, "The odds of dying in an earthquake are really low. Forest and Aria will be okay." She lets out a burst of air, her eyes focusing on mine, and it has me assuring her, "People have survived being trapped for days. They'll be okay."

She lifts a trembling hand and grabs hold of my shirt. Her shoulders jerk, and then she gasps for a breath of air.

I pull her to my chest, and when I wrap my arms around her, she begins to shiver from the shock.

"Shh... they're going to be okay," I say, trying my best to comfort her.

Carla suddenly pulls back and lifting her phone, she brings up Forest's number and presses dial. There's an automated response, and when her eyes dart up to mine, filled with fear, I say, "The cellphone towers could be knocked out. Communications are always first to go, along with power. This doesn't mean anything."

She nods, and grasping onto my words, she says, "You're right." She takes a shaky breath. "You're right." A tear spirals down her cheek, and I reach up to brush it off her skin. Then her voice sounds hoarse as she whispers, "You're right."

I pull her back to my chest and hold her tightly. "They'll be found soon."

Carla's shoulders shake, and she cries silently. I rub a hand over her back. I keep dropping kisses on her temple and hair.

Even though I know the stats, there's still the fear that Forest or Aria could be the one in twenty thousand.

God, please let me be right. Bring them safely home.

I take Carla back to the couch and sitting down, I pull her onto my lap and cradle her body against mine. Except for a shudder rippling through her every couple of minutes, she remains still in my arms.

I lift my hand to her face, and placing a finger beneath her chin, I nudge her up so she'll look at me. There are tear tracks on her cheeks, and the sight makes an aching feeling squeeze my heart. Using my thumb, I brush the wetness away. Our eyes lock, and feeling the need to reassure her, I say, "They're okay. We'll hear something soon."

Taking a deep breath, Carla nods. She lifts her arms and wraps them around my neck, and then she hugs me tightly. I hold her against me and press a kiss to her neck, trying to offer her comfort the only way I know how.

Chapter 11

CARLA

Waiting for news is torture. I keep alternating between fearing the worst and hoping my phone will ring any second to tell me Forest and Aria are okay.

My cold is totally forgotten as I try to remember my last words to them, but I can't. I can't recall what they wore when they left.

My eyes burn from staring at nothing, and my lips are dry from crying.

Noah stirs, and I feel his breath skim over my hair, then he says, "Let me call Kao."

I shift off his lap, and my muscles ache from sitting still so long. I check my phone for the hundredth time, and seeing no missed calls or texts, my heart sinks even deeper into a pit of despair.

I watch Noah dial Kao's number, then he clears his throat and says, "Hey, any news?" There's a moment's silence, and his eyes dart to me. "Yeah, we'll be there in a couple of minutes."

When he ends the call, he says, "Kao says everyone is heading to their place so we can be together while we wait for news. They haven't heard anything yet."

I nod and go to my room to put on shoes and grab a sweater. When I walk back into the living room, Noah takes my hand. He links our fingers as we walk out of the suite.

I feel relieved that we're going to Fallon's. Getting out of the suite makes me breathe a little easier.

The moment I see Fallon, the tears come again. I rush to her, and we hug each other tightly for a long moment. Knowing I have to be strong for her, I pull back and ask, "How are you holding up?"

She shakes her head, and with a quivering chin, she says, "I'm not. I'm going to lose my mind."

Jase comes in and walking right to us, he wraps his arms around both of us. "I just spoke with Uncle Mason. He says they've found a girl, but they need to dig through the rubble to get to her. Let's hope it's Aria."

"What about Forest?" Fallon gasps, her face crumbling with tears. "Oh God. Where's Forest?"

Just then her phone rings and she hurries to answer it. "Daddy?"

She listens for a moment, and then she begins to sob heartbreakingly.

No. No. No.

My blurring eyes are locked on her, and when she ends the call, she buries her face against Jase. "They think they've found him, but he seems to be unconscious. They're working on getting to them."

I feel a hand on my shoulder, and then Noah's chest presses against my back. He wraps his arms around the front of me and rests his chin on my head. Bringing my hands up, I grip hold of his forearms as I try to draw strength from him.

The air is tense and filled with worry. My stomach begins to burn from all the concern eating away at me.

When Hunter and Jade arrive, it feels like a grim shroud of death is dropped over all of us. We gather together in the living room, and as Noah sits down, he again pulls me onto his lap. I wrap my arms around his waist and rest my cheek against his shoulder. My gaze keeps drifting from Hana to Fallon and Kao, to Jase and Mila, to Hunter and Jade.

Fallon's phone begins to ring, and it has us all jerking from the sudden sound.

"Daddy?" Again she listens, and then her eyes drift closed, and a breath shudders from her. "Okay... okay... love you."

Before she can tell us what Uncle Falcon said, Hunter's phone rings.

"Aria!" Hunter darts up. "Are you okay?" He lifts a hand to his brow, and then he slumps back on the couch. "But you're okay?" He shuts his eyes and sucks in a deep breath. "I'm sure he'll be okay. I love you."

Jase's phone beeps, and then mine. I hurry to check the message.

Dad: Talking with Uncle Falcon. They've found Forest and Aria. Aria's fine. Forest has been rushed to the hospital, but he seems stable. Will call in a couple of minutes.

"They've found them," Jase says, and a collective sigh escapes around the room. "Forest has been taken to the hospital. He's stable, though. We'll know more soon."

We're all overwhelmed with relief, and I bury my face against Noah's neck as the emotions wash over me.

When we finally get the news that Forest has a broken arm and four broken ribs but that he's okay, I'm exhausted to my core.

It's as if the worry burned through all my energy.

"You should all stay the night," Kao says. "Grab a guest room or a couch. I'll put out some pillows and blankets."

Everyone leaves to find a spot to rest, then Noah says, "Want to crash here?"

I nod. "I'm good with anywhere." I get up and say, "I'm just going to get a glass of water. Do you want some?"

Noah shakes his head as he kicks off his shoes before stretching out on the couch.

When I come back from drinking water, I sit down on the other couch, and when I've taken off my sneakers, Noah murmurs, "Come over here."

I move to where Noah's lying, and he tugs at my hand, so I'll lie down. I crawl over him and positioning half my body over his, I rest my hand and cheek on his chest.

"Thank you, Noah."

He places a hand against my cheek, and then I feel him press a kiss to my hair. "Try to get some sleep."

I nod, and listening to his heartbeat, it doesn't take me long to drift off.

———————————————

NOAH

It's been a rough week for everyone, but Forest and Aria are finally back home. Forest has some healing to do, but at least they survived the disaster.

Walking into the living room, I see Carla's lying on one of the couches, watching Shrek with Forest and Aria. I drop down on the other open couch, and just as I get into the movie, Carla's face suddenly hovers above mine. She almost gives me a damn heart attack because she snuck up on me.

Then she impersonates *Donkey*, "I hate it when you've got somebody in your face, you trying to give them a hint, and they won't leave. Then there's that big awkward silence… you know…"

I struggle not to laugh as I stare up at her. She's so damn cute when she mimics an animation.

"Can I lie with you?" She even pulls an adorable face.

Teasing her, I grumble, "Nope."

Carla pouts down at me, and it fills me with the urge to kiss her. "Can I lie with you… Please."

"Fuck," I mutter because I can't kiss her right now. I continue teasing her, "You're not going to stop, are you?"

"Nope."

"Fine," I huff.

Carla comes to lie down half over me and rests her head on my chest. She lets out a happy sigh. "Not so bad, is it?"

I shake my head. "You're not the one being used for a pillow."

Then she snuggles into me. "My favorite pillow."

The now-familiar emotions ripple through me before I turn my gaze back to the TV.

I rest my arm over Carla and begin to brush my fingers over her arm, taking in the feel of her soft skin. We're not even halfway through the movie before she falls asleep with her fingers curled into my shirt.

I'm overly conscious of her body pressing against mine, and it makes need ripple through my abdomen. It's getting hard to take things slow with her. Then again, we've technically been dating a week. Not that we've done much dating with what happened to Forest and Aria.

When Shrek is almost done, I close my eyes and pretend I've fallen asleep as well. I listen as Forest and Aria turn off the TV and lights before they head toward the hallway. I wait a couple minutes longer, then I open my eyes again.

Now that we're alone, I shift a bit down, so I'm more comfortable and wrapping both my arms around Carla, I let out a contented sigh and drift off to sleep.

I feel the heat from her body as she lies half over me. My hand keeps trailing up and down her arm, her skin as soft as silk beneath my fingers.

Carla glances up at me, and seeing the desire in her eyes, my self-control is non-existent. Taking hold of her jaw, I crush my mouth to hers. Her moan reverberates into me as her hand moves from my chest, slipping under my sweatpants. Her fingers wrap around my cock, and she begins to stroke me, making my body go up in flames with need for her.

"Noah," she moans…

I wake up with one hell of a start, my heart pounding in my chest. It takes me a moment to realize I'm lying on the couch with Carla, and it was only a dream. Instantly disappointment wells in my chest because it felt so real… so good.

Carla stirs, pressing her body against mine, and her arm tightens around me.

My cock hardens to the point where it's bordering on painful. I have no doubt it would take only a matter of seconds for me to come if Carla were to wrap her fingers around my cock.

She pushes her body closer and moves her leg over mine, and it makes her thigh push against my cock. A burst of pleasure shoots through me, making my body jerk.

You want to take it slow with her.

You want to take it slow with her.

You want to…

Carla moves her thigh higher until she covers my cock, and it ceases all brain activity for me. She glances up at me, and she must see the desire on my face because she pushes herself up. When she straddles me and her pussy presses down on my cock, I grab hold of her hips.

Pleasure makes me stiff as fuck, and I can't stop myself from thrusting up against her, needing more friction.

Some brain activity returns, enough for me to mutter, "Even though we're in a relationship…" She rubs herself against my cock, making it impossible for me to finish my sentence.

"Yeah?" Carla places her hands on my jaw and leans closer. "What about it?"

She pushes down on me, and I only manage to moan, "I wanted…" I tighten my grip on her hips, "to take it slow."

Carla stops moving, and her eyes lock on mine. "Do you want to wait?"

"Not anymore. We…" Her mouth crashes against mine, and then I figure we're done talking.

Carla's tongue slips into my mouth, and I move my hand to the back of her neck as I tilt my head. Our lips work each other into a frenzy, hunger in every nip, every tug, every suck.

I can feel the heat from her pussy right through our clothes, and lowering one hand to her ass, I push myself up into a sitting position. Breaking the kiss, I say, "Wrap your legs around me."

Carla doesn't hesitate, and when I stand up with her in my arms, she begins to rain kisses down my neck until she sucks on my pulse. My fingers dig into her ass as I walk us to her room. I shut the door before carrying her over to the bed. When I lay her down, our eyes lock. The heat in her gaze makes me lose my mind, and the need to consume her overwhelms me.

I push my hand inside her sweatpants and panties, and cupping her pussy, I growl, "Do you want this?"

Carla nods, and she instantly begins to rub her clit against my palm.

I massage her, taking in the feel of her warm skin, and it's intoxicating. I lean into her and bite her bottom lip before sucking on it. Then I ask, "Are you sure because once I start, I won't be able to stop?"

She reaches for my shirt, muttering, "I've waited years for this. If you ask me one more time if I want it, I'm tying you to the bed."

I pull my hand free from her pants and help her take off my shirt. While I drop the fabric to the floor, Carla yanks her own t-shirt over her head.

I unclasp her bra and then grab hold of her hands. Pushing them down on the mattress above her head, I tie the fabric around her wrists. Bringing my gaze back to hers, I murmur, "Don't try to free your hands and keep them there. I'm going to take my time exploring every inch of you."

Carla nods, her breaths already coming fast over her parted lips.

I move my arm under her back and lift her from the bed. Her breasts rub against my skin, and it causes a rush of blood to surge through my heart. I shift her up the mattress before laying her back down, and then I slip my fingers into her waistband and pull her sweatpants and panties down her legs.

When I have her naked, I kneel between her legs and sit back so I can admire her body. Her plump breasts and pebbled nipples beg me to suck them. Her curves make my hands itch, and the V between her legs makes my cock harden until it feels like I might explode.

The emotions feel primal, and I'm consumed with the need to dominate and worship her.

Chapter 12

CARLA

My eyes are locked on Noah as emotions flash over his face, and then a controlling look tightens his features. It makes my abdomen clench with anticipation.

Holy shit, I've waited so long for this, and now that it's happening, it's surreal.

Noah takes hold of my thighs and pushes my legs wide open. I don't feel self-conscious as his eyes burn over my clit and entrance.

I have no idea what to expect from him. I've had sex twice, with Claudio, my first boyfriend. Actually, he was my only boyfriend, and I was too young to fully understand what I was doing.

Noah's gaze trails up my body until they lock on mine. "Are you a virgin?" I shake my head, and it makes a frown form on his forehead. "When?"

"Before I fell in love with you," I whisper. "I was fourteen."

His frown darkens until he looks pissed off. "We'll talk about that later."

I nod quickly.

He crawls over me, keeping himself braced on his hands and knees, and then he lowers his head, and he presses a tender kiss to my lips. As my lips part to allow him inside my mouth, he pulls back.

I begin to frown, but then he settles back between my legs. His thighs press against my ass, and it lifts my hips off the bed.

Noah brings a hand to my cheek, and his touch is feather soft as he brushes his fingers down to my neck. His eyes follow his hand as he continues down to my breast. When his fingertips skim over my nipple, my back arches, wanting more.

He keeps going over my ribs and abdomen, and his touch is frustratingly restrained when he reaches my clit.

"Noah," I groan, needing more. So much more.

"Shh..." His eyes lock on mine again as he softly circles my opening.

Finally, he pushes his middle finger inside me, but too quickly, he pulls back out. My body begins to tremble as he lifts his finger to his mouth, and when he sucks on it, heat pools in my core.

Holy hotness.

"I know you need to process things, but can you process my body after you've fucked me," I complain.

A too hot smirk tugs at his lips as he slowly shakes his head. "I need to be in control."

My body writhes with frustration. "But it's torture."

Noah places his hands on the outside of my thighs, and as he rubs his palms up toward my hips, he murmurs, "That's the idea." He keeps moving up my body until he cups both my breasts, squeezing them lightly.

I arch into his touch and groan, "To torture me?"

He nods as he leans over me, and then his mouth closes over my nipple. I lift my hips, my clit hot and aching for friction, but Noah grabs hold of my sides and pushes me back down onto the mattress as his teeth tug my nipple.

Noah is everything I've ever wanted. With his mouth on my breast, emotion begins to build in my chest, but I push it down, needing to focus on every single thing he does.

His fingers curl into my hips, and for a moment, his touch is firm, but then it lessens again, drawing a frustrated groan from me.

He lets go of my nipple and presses a kiss to my neck, and then he pulls back. His gaze moves over my skin, making me feel hot and needy. One of his hands moves in between my legs, and the pad of his finger again brushes softly over my clit. This time Noah keeps stroking me until the slight touch just about drives me insane.

"You have too much patience," I growl. Shooting him a glare, I threaten, "I'm a second away from jumping you."

Again his mouth curves into a sinful smirk.

He knows exactly what he's doing to me, and he's enjoying it.

I should've known Noah would be dominating in bed, seeing as he's controlling in every other aspect of his life. The thought makes me submit, and my body relaxes into the mattress.

The moment I do, Noah notices, and his smirk grows into a pleased smile. "I wondered how long you would try to fight me."

He moves down on the bed, and then his hands grip hold of my hips. The moment his teeth scrape over my clit, my mouth drops open, and my body convulses.

"Noah," I gasp as intense sensations flood my body and tighten my abdomen, drawing a whimper from me.

He begins to devour me, and it only increases the tightening in my core until it feels as if I might snap at any moment. Unable to keep still, I bring my hands to his hair.

The instant I touch Noah, he stops and shakes his head at me. "Hands back where they belong."

I let out a groan but do as he says, and it earns me a grin before his head ducks low, and he sucks hard at my clit.

I lose control over my body as I begin to convulse, and then an intense orgasm spasms through me. It feels as if I'm being electrocuted by pleasure until all my nerves hum like live wires.

NOAH

Watching Carla come apart is the most beautiful sight I've ever seen, and it fills me with a sense of possessiveness.

I've never wanted to possess anything until this moment. Watching her lips part as her breaths explode from her, her body quivering, and her hips grinding down on my hand as she rides out her pleasure – makes me stare in amazement.

Her reaction to me makes satisfaction warm my chest.

Moving off the bed, I step out of my sweatpants. Carla's eyes drift over my body until she gets to my cock. She stares while biting her lower lip.

I crawl over her, and using my thumb, I pull her lip free from between her teeth, and then I crush my mouth to hers. I pour everything she's made me feel over the past couple of weeks into the kiss. My tongue caresses hers with hard strokes, and my teeth knead her lips.

When I break the kiss, her lips are swollen, and her eyelashes are lowered. I move back until I'm kneeling between her legs. Taking hold of my cock, I brush the head over her clit, and the sensations rippling through me almost makes me lose control.

I pause for a moment, and when my eyes go to Carla's face, I see that she's watching me. I rub my cock over her again and watch as she holds her breath. When I pull back, she exhales.

Glancing down, I position my cock at her entrance. I take hold of her hips and push the head inside. Seeing how she stretches for me makes heat sizzle up my spine.

My gaze locks on Carla's face as I push in a little deeper. Emotion washes over her features as if she's about to cry, and it makes me move over her until I'm bracing myself with my forearms resting on either side of her head.

Our eyes lock, and her longing and love for me are laid bare in her irises. I push deeper inside her and then press a tender kiss to her mouth. Lifting my head, our eyes meet again, and then I thrust all the way into her. Her lips part on a gasp, and it takes a moment for her to adjust to having my cock inside her. Then a pleading look tightens her features as she murmurs, "I want to touch you."

I reach for her wrists and loosen the fabric, freeing her hands. She instantly brings them to my jaw, and lifting her head, her mouth presses against mine. I let her take control of the kiss.

I don't move while our tongues dance together. When Carla ends the kiss, I pull my cock out before thrusting back inside her.

Her eyes never leave mine as she flattens her palms on my chest, and she explores the dips and swells of my torso.

Only when her hands move to my back, do I pull out again. I pause for a second, and then I drive back into her.

Every time I fill Carla, her pupils dilate more, and her breaths come a little faster.

She lifts her legs and wrap them around my ass, making me sink deeper inside her.

Using one arm to keep my upper body raised above her, I move my other hand to her breast and drink in the feel of her soft skin as I massage her hard nipple.

My hips begin to move with short but hard thrusts, keeping my pace slow. Carla lets out a whimper and turns her head to my bicep. Her teeth sink into my skin as her body arches against mine.

I'm so absorbed by her reactions to my cock thrusting inside her that I don't take in how fast my heart is beating or how shallow and quick my breaths are bursting over my lips.

In this intimate moment, there's only Carla.

I pull out until only the head of my cock is inside her, and then I drive back into her, hard and fast.

"Ah... Noah," she moans. Her head tilts back, exposing her throat to me as her arms move to the covers, and she grabs fistfuls of the silky fabric. Her legs slip away from me, and her thighs fall open for me.

With her body surrendering to me, I drop my hand to her hip and tightening my hold, I begin to thurst harder, picking up my pace. Pleasure begins to spasm down my spine, and it makes me pound into her.

A throaty moan escapes Carla before her body begins to convulse in my hold. Crushing my mouth to hers, my hips hammer against hers as I chase my own orgasm.

The release is intense, making my cock feel sensitive as her inner walls grip me tightly. Breaking the kiss, I let out a gasp, and then I'm unable to draw another breath as my body jerks against Carla's. I drop my forehead to her shoulder as the overwhelming pleasure strips me of my control.

When the last of our orgasms shudder through us, my body slumps against Carla's. My breath rushes over my lips, and it takes me a long moment before I finally have the strength to lift myself up.

My eyes find Carla's, and I watch as a tear rolls into her hair.

She brings her hands to my jaw, and lifting her head, she presses a tender kiss to my lips. Then she whispers, "I love you, Noah."

This time I get to soak in the warmth of her words as they fold around my heart.

I'm not yet at the point where I can say the words back to her and instead kiss her before I murmur, "Thank you for never giving up on my stubborn ass."

A smile spreads over her face. "Never. You're stuck with me for life."

My lips curve up. "Lucky me."

Chapter 13

CARLA

When I come out of the bathroom, wearing my t-shirt and panties, I expect to find the bed empty. A burst of happiness flutters through me when I see Noah leaning back against a stack of pillows, with a sheet pulled over his lower half. My eyes drink in the sight of his chest and abs.

Eye-porn at its best.

"I can get used to seeing you in my bed," I tease as I climb in next to him.

His eyes meet mine, and the dominant look he had while we made love has receded behind his hazel irises. Just thinking about it makes me hot and bothered again.

He lifts his arm, and I snuggle into his side. When his fingers begin to brush up and down my arm, he says, "I wanted to take it much slower."

I let out a chuckle.

Staring at my dresser, Noah clears his throat, and then he asks, "I didn't traumatize you, did I?"

My eyes dart to his as I sit up beside him. "Why would you ask that?"

His eyes slowly meet mine. "My need to be in control."

Instantly a grin spreads over my face. "It was hot. Like supernova hot."

The corner of his mouth lifts before a serious expression tightens his features. "Please tell me you're on the pill."

I widen my eyes and pretend to be worried, but then let out a burst of laughter. "I am."

Noah relaxes visibly. "With that out of the way, let's talk about you losing your virginity at fourteen. What the fuck?"

"Yeah, not my proudest moment," I mutter as I begin to draw patterns on the mattress. "It was a mistake."

"Who with? How old was he?" His voice sounds low and... deadly, as if he wants to kill Claudio for daring to touch me.

Tilting my head, a soft smile tugs at my lips. I lift my hand to Noah's jaw. "I love your protective side, but it was my fault as well. I said yes." Dropping my hand, I shrug. "I was young and stupid."

"How old was he?" Noah bites the question out.

"Seventeen."

Noah shakes his head, a frown forming between his eyes. "The fucker. Who was it? Give me a name."

I shift closer to Noah and give him a pleading look. "It's in the past. Can we just forget about it?"

Noah lets out a heavy breath. "You were fourteen, Carla. God, that's statutory rape."

"Not to me." He still looks like he could kill someone. "Noah," I whisper. When his eyes lock on mine, I continue, "It didn't mean anything. It was a mistake."

He takes a deep breath, and reaching for my hand, he links our fingers. "Was he the only one?"

My eyes sharpen on Noah's face, and when I realize he wants to know if I've been faithful to my love for him, my lips curve up. "When I fell in love with you, it was the end of me dating. Yes, I flirted, but no guy ever compared to you."

My answer makes a pleased smile form on his lips, then he asks, "Do you masturbate?"

My eyebrows dart up, and I feel my cheeks flush, but I still nod and tease him, "It might traumatize you to learn how many fantasies you've starred in."

"Yeah?" Noah murmurs as he lifts a hand to the back of my neck. He pulls me closer, and his lips skim over mine. "I want to see your toys."

I let out a burst of laughter. "You're leaning against them."

He pulls a little back, a hot smirk settling on his face. "Pillows?"

I nod.

"Yeah?" He leans closer to me, and his teeth tug at my bottom lip, sending a rush of tingles through my body. "Do you rub yourself against them?"

I nod against his mouth.

His tongue skims over my lips, and as I open for him, he murmurs, "What do you fantasize about?"

I slip my tongue into his mouth as my body moves forward. I wrap my arms around his neck as I straddle him. Feeling how hard he is for me sends a tremble through me.

"I can show you," I moan against his lips, filled with need for him.

Noah's hands settle on my hips. His eyes pin mine, and I watch as he contemplates giving me control, then he murmurs, "Did you picture me naked?"

His question makes heat pool in my abdomen. I take a deep breath before I nod.

Desire darkens his eyes, and his fingers curl into my skin. "Show me how badly you wanted my cock inside you."

Holy. Shit.

No fantasy I've ever had could prepare me for the real thing.

I move off the bed, and taking hold of my panties, I push them down my legs. I grab hold of the sheet and pull it away from Noah, exposing his hard cock to me.

Just as well, I took off my panties because they would've gone up in flames at the sight of Noah's body.

Absolute perfection.

My gaze meets his. "I can do anything?"

He nods.

I climb back over him, and the second my clit rubs over his hard length, a delicious shiver rushes through me.

I place my hands on his jaw, and leaning forward, I press a kiss to his mouth. As my tongue slips inside his mouth, my palms move down, drinking in the feel of his muscled chest. You'd swear the man was carved from granite. All hard dips and swells.

My hips begin to swivel, and I grind myself over his cock.

Noah lifts a hand to the back of my neck, and tilting his head, he takes control of the kiss. It quickly turns into a dirty hot mess, making me rub harder against him.

His other hand grips hold of my ass, his touch biting at my skin.

Suddenly he growls, "This fantasy better include penetration, or we'll have to work on your imagination."

"Patience," I whisper against his lips.

NOAH

Patience is not something I have when she's riding my cock like it's a mastered skill. She shouldn't be this good with her lack of experience.

The thought makes me break the kiss and ask, "How did you get so good at this?"

Carla's pussy keeps sliding over my cock, her movements sensual and hot as fuck.

"Many…" her teeth tugs at my bottom lip, "many nights of fantasizing."

"How often," I hiss as her ass brushes over my balls.

"Depends," she murmurs. Her eyes meet mine, and they're dark with desire. "If you did something I liked, I humped the hell out of that pillow. If you made me angry, it ended up in the corner of the room."

Her answer makes me grin.

"But then there was makeup sex afterward."

She presses down hard on me, and her hips begin to move faster, making me hiss, "Yeah?"

"Yeah," she moans. She takes hold of my hands and places them over her breasts. I hate that she's still wearing the t-shirt. Covering my hands with hers, she forces me to touch her hard. My fingers dig into the fabric, and I squeeze her breasts together until a deep cleavage peeks from the shirt's collar. I pull the fabric down until it's under her breasts, pushing them up.

"I'm going to fuck your breasts," I growl, and the thought makes my cock jerk against her.

"Noah," she whimpers, and it kills me to not take over.

Carla grinds down on me, and her movements become jerky as her body tightens. Mesmerized, I watch as her lips part, and her eyes drift closed. She lets out a breathy moan, "Ah... God, I'm going to come..." She tilts her head back as her body convulses from the orgasm rippling through her. "Yes... Fuck, Noah."

It's the same as when she had to fake the orgasm for the fear pong.

The instant her eyes open and they focus on me, I growl, "You will never do that for a dare again."

She nods as she begins to move down my legs. My gaze locks on her as her hand closes around the base of my cock, and the moment her mouth sucks me into her wet heat, I know I'm not going to last long.

Both my hands move into her hair, and I grab fistfuls of her silky strands as her mouth begins to work my cock into a fucking frenzy of heat and lust.

Tightening my grip on her hair, I begin to thrust into her mouth while biting out, "Grip me harder. Let me feel your nails."

She tightens her hold on my cock, threatening to squeeze the orgasm out of me.

Her teeth scrape over the sensitive head, and when she sucks me so hard, her cheeks hollow out, and her eyes lift to mine, intense pleasure rips a grunt from me. My cock begins to jerk in her mouth as my orgasm seizes my body.

Once she's swallowed the last drop, I drag her up my body and crush my mouth to hers. I suck hard on her tongue before I pull back and ask, "That's your fantasy?"

"One of them," she says, a satisfied gleam in her eyes. "It's going to take us a while to work through them all."

I let out a chuckle as I lock her against my chest in a tight hug. "You're full of surprises."

Carla snuggles against me, asking, "Just, so there are no misunderstandings… we're officially a couple now? Right?"

Taking hold of her jaw, I lift her face to mine, and I pin her with a scowl. "Yes, so I better not catch you flirting with some sackless dickhead."

A wide smile spreads over her face. "You realize what this means, right?"

"We're dating?" I grumble.

Carla shakes her head. "I won."

A burst of laughter escapes me. "Yeah? Are you happy with your prize?"

A loving look softens her features. "You have no idea how happy I am." Pushing herself closer to me, she presses a kiss to my mouth. "All I ever wanted was to love you."

My eyes caress her face as warmth spreads through my heart. "Mine," I whisper before I claim her lips in a possessive kiss.

Chapter 14

CARLA

The Noah I thought I knew and the Noah I'm getting to know – yeah, two totally different people.

Holy shit.

We were up half the night, either talking or making love. I can still feel him between my legs.

When I walk into the kitchen, Mila, Hana, and Forest are already having coffee.

"Morning," I grin at them. I fix myself a cup of coffee, then turn to face them before I drop the bomb, "Noah and I are officially dating."

Three equally stunned faces stare back at me. Mila's the first to find her voice. "Wow. I so did not see that coming."

Cocking my head to the side, I ask, "Why?"

Mila shakes her head, and just as Noah comes into the kitchen, she answers, "He's not actually the dating kind."

Noah grips hold of my jaw, and he presses a hard kiss to my lips before he takes the cup from my hands to take a sip. He hands my coffee back to me, then smiles at our friends. "That's before Carla wore me down."

Forest lets out a sputter of laughter, almost choking on his coffee. Clearing his throat, he says, "I warned you once Carla sets her sights on something, she doesn't stop."

"Yeah, that's what I like most about her," Noah chuckles. His phone beeps, and I watch as he reads the message, then he mutters, "Fuck."

My eyes lock on him as he dials a number, and then turning away from us, he says to whoever he called, "Are you okay?" He walks down the hallway, and the last I hear is, "If you couldn't save him, no one could."

"His mom," Mila whispers. "She probably lost a patient."

"Oh," I gasp. I finish my coffee and rinse my cup. "Have a good day, everyone," I say as I walk down the hallway to Noah's room.

I hesitate by his door, not sure if I should knock first or if I can just go in.

The door swings open, and the moment Noah's eyes land on me, he grabs hold of my wrist and yanks me inside. He shuts the door, and then his body presses hard against mine as he shoves me against the wood. His mouth crashes down on mine, and he kisses me as if he's been starving for the taste of me.

I lift my hands to the back of his head, and my fingers get lost in his hair as our tongues duel for control.

When he finally pulls back, we're both breathless. He presses his forehead to mine as we take a moment to come down from the high of the kiss.

I clear my throat and ask, "Are you okay?"

He nods. "My mom just takes it hard whenever she loses someone."

I wrap my arms around Noah's neck and hug him as tight as I can.

He slips an arm around my waist, and his other hand grips hold of my ass. Then he grumbles, "God, I want to fuck you right now."

I let out a chuckle. "I'm still recovering from last night, and we need to get to our classes."

He pulls back, and his gaze locks with mine while a hot smirk tugs at the corner of his mouth. "Yeah? Are you sore?"

"Just tender."

His hand moves to my front and slips between my legs, then he cups me lightly. "Good. That way, you'll be reminded of my cock inside you all day long."

I shake my head. "I underestimated you, Noah West."

"Now you understand why I pushed you away," he murmurs.

I nod. "I do."

He tilts his head. "Do you still want to be with me?"

I bring my hands to his jaw, and feeling the sharp edges causes a fluttering in my stomach. "More than anything."

My words earn me another pleased smile from Noah. He cups me hard between my legs before he pulls his hand away. Reaching for the doorknob, he says, "Let's get to class."

I place my hand against the door, then ask, "Can I ask you a question?"

"Sure."

"Mila said you never dated. Is that true?"

Noah's eyes drift over my face. "I tried a couple of times, but it never lasted."

His answer piques my curiosity. "Why?"

"Because I struggle with the emotional side of a relationship."

His answer makes a frown form on my brow. "But you've been fine with me."

Noah shakes his head, and his mouth curves up. "You're patient with me. You give me the time to process what I'm feeling where the others didn't bother." Noah takes a step closer to me, and he presses a tender kiss to my lips. "It's like you know exactly when to push and when to wait. Besides my family, Kao's the only one who understands me like that."

I grin up at him. "I'm glad to hear that."

He opens the door. "We better get going, or we'll be late."

My heart feels as light as a feather as we leave his room. When we walk out of the suite, Noah wraps his arm around my shoulders and yanks me tightly to his side.

NOAH

The past week of being in a relationship with Carla has been surprising. It's definitely not what I expected. There are no demands, no arguments about me not telling her I love her back. No angry glares because I haven't bought her anything or made a huge fuss over her.

Carla's happy with me just as I am, and it makes me want to do everything for her that I hated doing for any of my ex-girlfriends.

I realize it's because I hate being told what to do. Carla's letting me take the lead where the others tried to lead me.

I now understand why the emotions I feel for Carla scared and confused the hell out of me in the beginning. It's because I knew it would give her power over me, and I didn't like the idea one bit.

Turns out, that's not the case.

With every happy smile, every cuddle into my side, and every moan drifting over her lips, Carla is making me fall in love with her – deeply, irrevocably, and fast.

For the first time in my life, I struggle to focus on the lectures. No article can keep my attention.

There's only Carla.

The instant the lecture is over, I'm up and out of my seat. I grab my bag and flinging it over my shoulder, I stalk out of the class. Pulling my phone from my pocket, I text Carla.

N: Where are you right now?"

Seconds later, she types out a reply.

C: I just finished at the library and walking toward the restaurant.

Another couple of seconds later.

C: Passing the parking area.

A grin tugs at my lips as she keeps typing.

C: Passing the dorms.

She comes into my line of sight, and I shove the device back in my pocket as I walk toward her. When I'm within touching distance of Carla, her head snaps toward me, and then a beautiful smile spreads over her face. I grab hold of the back of her neck and crush my mouth to hers.

Dropping my bag to the sidewalk, I bring my hand to her back and press her against me as I kiss her with every realization I've had about us.

The little girl who used to annoy the shit out of me has become the epitome of love. She is the most real thing I have ever felt in my entire life.

She's the other half of my soul.

I pull back, and my eyes lock on hers.

She must see something on my face because she asks, "What? Did something happen?"

I shake my head as everything I feel for her fills my heart to the brim, and then I murmur, "I love you."

Carla blinks at me, and then she whispers, "What did you just say?"

My lips curve up as I take in her shocked expression. Lifting my hands, I frame her face. I press a tender kiss to her parted lips, then repeat the words. "I love you, Carla."

Watching the words take root inside her is like watching a flower bloom. Then in typical Carla-style, she lets out a shriek, and throwing her arms around my neck, she bounces with happiness.

Carla stills, and she tightens her hold on me as her body jerks. "Oh my God, Noah. Thank you," she whimpers against my neck. "Thank you for loving me back."

I wrap her against me and press a kiss to her temple.

When she pulls back, she wipes happy tears from her face.

"Why the fuck are you crying?" Jase suddenly growls near us, startling the shit out of us.

"I got good news," Carla says, smiling at her brother. "What are you doing here?"

"I'm here to pick up Mila." Jase's eyes snap to me, then he says, "Can I have a moment alone with Noah?"

Carla places her hands on her sides, and tilting her head, she scowls at Jase. "No, you cannot. Whatever you have to say to him, you can say in front of me."

148

I have to suppress a grin at her spitfire attitude.

"Fine," Jase huffs. He crosses his arms over his chest as his gaze locks on mine. "Imagine my surprise when I just saw you kissing my little sister. Care to explain?"

I wrap an arm around Carla's shoulders and pull her against my side, all while not breaking eye contact with Jase. "We're dating."

Jase's eyebrow lifts slightly, then he grumbles, "Are you now?"

Knowing how protective Jase is of Carla, I say, "I love her. I'll take good care of her. You have nothing to worry about."

He stares a moment longer at me, and then his features relax because he knows I won't just say those words if I don't mean them.

The corner of his mouth begins to lift. "You know how lucky you are to have her, right?"

My mouth curves up. "Yes, I do."

Jase looks at Carla. "I'm impressed."

"Why?" She frowns at him.

"You didn't settle for a guy you could walk all over," Jase explains.

"Pfft," Carla huffs. "Where's the fun in that?"

Jase bursts out laughing, then he gestures to the restaurant. "Let me just find Mila, then we can have an early dinner together."

"Sure," I answer on our behalf.

Chapter 15

CARLA

There are no words to describe how happy I am. The only wish I ever had is coming true. It's been ten days since Noah and I became official, and every moment with him is still surreal.

Whenever I walk into a room, and he's there, butterflies erupt in my stomach. For a split-second, I'll hesitate, the old feelings of having to keep my distance from him surfacing. But then his eyes will lock on mine, and they'll fade.

Noah's mine. I can touch him at any time. I can kiss him.

Walking into the library, I whisper a line from *The Little Mermaid*, "Who says that my dreams have to stay just my dreams."

A soft smile plays around my mouth as I set my bag down by an empty table, and glancing around, I notice

Noah sitting a couple of tables away from me. My gaze takes him in as he concentrates on what he's reading.

Damn, he's hot.

I let out a happy sigh and go get the books I'll need on ethics. I set them down on the wooden surface as I take a seat. Opening my laptop, I glance at Noah, and when I see him leaning back in his chair, watching me, I grin at him.

I try to focus on my work but feeling Noah's eyes on me makes it near impossible. I glance at him again, and it makes the corner of his mouth lift.

I begin to contemplate whether I should ditch getting my work done when a girl approaches Noah.

I lean back in my chair, ready to enjoy the show, as she sits down in the chair next to him.

I wish I could hear what she's saying, but she seems to be whispering. Noah shakes his head, and it makes her pull a pleading face. Then he nods in my direction, and she turns her head toward me.

I lift a hand and wave my fingers at her. "The position of annoying talking animal has already been taken," I impersonate *Donkey* from *Shrek*.

She darts up and giving me an apologetic look, she walks away as fast as she can.

When my eyes find Noah's, he winks at me as laughter shakes his shoulders.

Blowing him a kiss, I try to focus on my assignment. Suddenly someone shuts my laptop, and as I glance up, Noah murmurs, "Follow me."

I'm just about to argue when I see the dominant look darkening his irises. Knowing what it means, I swallow my words, and rising to my feet, I follow Noah to the back of the library.

He opens the door to a storage room, and once I've stepped inside, he shuts it behind me.

Taking a step closer to me, Noah's hands drop to my thighs, and his fingers trail up my skin and under my dress. His head ducks low, and his mouth claims mine. His scent envelops me as his lips work me into a frenzy. One of his hands grips hold of my butt while his other slips between my legs. He shoves my panties aside and then begins to rub my clit hard. I grab hold of his neck as my moans are muted by his mouth.

It doesn't take him long to make me come, and my body leans into him as my legs go numb for a moment.

I gasp against his lips as I come down from the orgasm. Noah fixes my panties before he presses a tender kiss to my mouth.

Grinning with satisfaction, I ask, "What was that for?"

Noah's eyes drift over my face. "For not assuming things and getting jealous when Amber came to talk to me."

"I trust you," I say. "You know that right?"

His lips curve up. "I do now."

When Noah opens the door, I check that my dress is right before following him back to my table.

This time he sits down next to me, and taking out his phone, he begins to read something.

I manage to work for an hour before Noah's hand settles on my back. He leans over me, and I feel his breath skim against my ear when he whispers, "I'll see you for dinner at six." He presses a kiss to my temple and then walks away.

NOAH

Dressed in charcoal cargo pants and a white button-up shirt, I make my way to the restaurant.

As always, I ignore the other patrons while walking to our table. One glance can lead to a conversation, which is the last thing I want. Before I take a seat, I remove the small box from my pocket and set it down on the pristine white tablecloth.

Checking my watch, I see Carla should be here soon.

A waiter comes to the table, and I place an order for two glasses of fruit juice.

When the waiter leaves, I lean back in the chair and picking up the box, I open it. My lips curve as I stare at the earrings. They're in the shape of half a heart with a diamond set in the curve. It was a part of the 'Epitome of Love' collection from Tiffany's.

Who would've thought Carla would be the one?

Certainly not me.

I let out a chuckle at my thoughts.

Over the past couple of weeks, I've fallen in love with all her quirks, which used to annoy me.

"Carla," I hear someone call, and my eyes dart up. I watch as she stops at a table where Kennedy is sitting, and then she shakes her head and gesture in my direction.

My gaze scans over the other tables, and I notice how guys drool over what's mine, especially Adam-the-dipshit.

I close the box and tuck it in my pocket as I rise to my feet. I stalk to where Carla's standing, and feeling an overwhelming need to stake my claim, I take hold of the back of her neck. Carla's head whips in my direction, and then I crush my mouth to hers. I brand her with my lips before I pull back.

I shoot a glare around the restaurant, then settle my gaze on Adam, growling, "Back the fuck off. She's mine."

Carla lets out a burst of laughter, and when I turn my attention back to her, she pats my chest, murmuring, "Caveman much?"

"Not even close," I reply as I take her hand and pull her to our table. "I couldn't very well fuck you in front of everyone." I pull out her chair so she can sit down, and then I take my seat next to her. "Did you get all your work done?"

"Yeah, thank God," Carla lets out a sigh as she pulls a menu closer. We decide what we want to eat and place our order when they bring our drinks.

Carla leans back in her chair, and her eyes scan slowly over my face.

Reaching up, I brush some strands away from her face, then ask, "What are you thinking right now?"

The corner of her mouth lifts. "How happy I am. It's still surreal at times that we're dating."

I tilt my head, our gazes locking. Knowing she needs to hear the words, I murmur, "I love you, Carla."

A dazzling smile graces her lips. "Say it again."

I lean closer to her until my mouth brushes against her ear, then I whisper, "I. Love. You." Pulling back, I take the box from my pocket and place it down on the table. "I got you something."

Carla's gaze darts to the box, and then she frowns. "Really? A gift?"

I nod and watch as she carefully opens the lid, and then her lips part on a gasp. "They're stunning." Her eyes dart to me. "But why?"

"Because I wanted to," I say as I lean back against my chair.

"Thank you, Noah." Carla removes the diamond studs she's wearing and puts on the new set. She closes the distance between us and presses a kiss to my mouth. "I love them."

"Yeah?" I murmur as she pulls back.

She nods, a euphoric expression on her face.

Lifting my hand, I brush my fingers over the line of her jaw while my gaze drinks in every inch of her face.

We stare at each other for the longest while, then Carla says, "Tell me something about you, I don't know."

I let out a chuckle. "That's impossible, seeing as you stalked my ass. I'm starting to think you know me better than I know myself."

Letting out a burst of laughter, Carla shakes her head. "I didn't know you were a caveman. I'm pretty sure there's more I don't know."

My phone beeps, and glancing at the screen, I see it's a message from my mother. Opening the text, I turn the device so Carla can read what Mom sent. "This is what I'm always reading on my phone."

Mom: I did an anatomical segmental resection today. Basically, I removed a cancerous tumor, the blood vessels, the lymphatic drainage, and the lung segment where the tumor was located. The patient is in recovery and responding well. How's your day?

Carla's eyes scan over the words, then she looks at me. "I'm going to pretend I know what your mom's talking about."

I let out a chuckle and reply to Mom.

N: I'm proud of you. My day was good. I'm having dinner with Carla. TTYL.

Turning my attention to Carla, I say, "My mom's medical journal entries have been my bedtime stories since I can remember."

Carla scrunches her nose. "No wonder your IQ is so high."

I move my hand to her leg and begin to caress my fingers up and down her inner thigh's soft skin. "Tell me something about you, I don't know."

"My grandfather and I read the same books, then discuss them once a week," she whispers, her breathing speeding up a little.

"Yeah? What are you reading now?"

Carla opens the kindle app on her phone and shows me the cover of the book. "*You Do You* by *Sarah Knight*," I read the title. "How is it?"

"Inspirational," she answers. "Thought-provoking." Her eyes smile into mine. "Kinda like you."

Her words make me close the distance between us, and I press a tender kiss to her lips.

Chapter 16

CARLA

I've been studying all morning and afternoon, and exhausted, I shove the laptop aside and lie back on the bed.

Damn, I could sleep for a week.

I snuggle into my pillow and figure I'll just close my eyes for a couple of minutes.

"Carla," I hear Noah murmur.

I let out a groan, then mumble, "I just finished studying. Give me a couple of minutes, and I'll be up."

Noah places his hand on my forehead, then asks, "Do you feel sick?"

I pry my eyes open. "No, I just want to nap."

His eyes scan over my face, a concerned look tightening his features. "You've been sleeping since yesterday afternoon."

I shoot up, gasping, "What?"

"It's Sunday. Eleven in the morning," he states.

"Nooooo!" I glance around for my laptop. "I needed to study. Why did I sleep so much?"

Noah frames my face with his hands and makes me look at him. "Are you sure you feel okay?"

I nod. "I'm just tired. It feels like I haven't slept at all." I begin to scoot off the bed. "I need to make up for the hours I missed."

Noah rises to his feet and then locks his fingers around my hand. "Shower. Eat. Then you can study. I'll help you catch up."

I let out a sigh. "Okay." I move closer and wrap my arms around his waist. Closing my eyes, I rest my cheek against his chest. "God, I could sleep just standing like this."

His arms move around me, and he holds me tightly. "After the exam tomorrow, you can sleep all you want."

I nod, and pulling away, I walk to my closet to get clean clothes.

"What do you feel like eating?" Noah asks.

Not hungry at all, I say, "Something light. A salad or soup?"

Noah's eyebrow pops up. "You want soup? Now I'm really getting worried."

I let out a chuckle. "I'm not hungry, that's all."

"I'll get you some Hydralyte to drink. The electrolytes will help boost your energy."

I give him a thankful smile before I walk into the bathroom. After I'm done showering, I brush my teeth and get dressed.

When I walk into the kitchen, Noah says, "Drink this. The food should be here soon." He watches me like a hawk as I swallow the electrolytes down.

I rinse the glass then grin at him. "How was your Saturday night?"

He lets out a burst of air as a smile tugs at his lips. "I spent the night watching you sleep."

My grin widens. "Yeah? Must've been boring."

He shakes his head and slowly moves closer to me. "Not at all." Wrapping his arm around my lower back, his other hand comes to my jaw. He lifts my face and presses a soft kiss to my mouth. Pulling back an inch, his eyes scan over my features. "Even though you were right there, I still missed you."

Lifting my arms, I let my fingers tangle with his hair. I close the distance between us, but the moment our mouths touch, Noah takes control of the kiss until I'm breathless and contemplating ditching my studies for some sexy time between the sheets.

A knock at the door pulls us apart. While Noah sets the food down on the kitchen island, I get us fruit juice from the fridge.

Taking a seat on a stool, I say, "I like that you drink juice as well."

Noah smiles as he places the bowl of chicken soup down in front of me. "Eat it all."

"Yes, Mr. West," I grumble playfully.

Noah tilts his head, his eyes sharpening on my face with a look of warning. "Don't say things like that if you want to study today."

Letting out a chuckle, I scoop up some soup and begin to eat.

After we're done eating, Noah spends the rest of the day, helping me get all the work crammed into my brain. He teaches me a new way to study, and it makes remembering points so much easier.

It's after midnight when I finally close my laptop, mumbling, "I should've asked for your notes instead of Jase's."

Noah lets out a chuckle as he stretches out next to me. "I don't have any notes."

"Right," I grumble as I snuggle into his side. Glancing up at him, I ask, "Will you sleep here tonight?"

Noah's eyes meet mine for a moment, then he says, "Sure, but I need to shower first."

He presses a kiss to my forehead before he gets up to go to his room.

I lie and stare at the ceiling for a couple of minutes before I get up to grab a fresh pair of shorts and a t-shirt. Sneaking out of my room, I dart to Noah's bedroom and quickly let myself in.

I can hear water running in the bathroom, and placing my clothes on his bed, I quickly get undressed. I go into the bathroom, and shutting the door softly, I stand and watch as Noah rinses suds from his hair.

My eyes drift over his muscled frame, and seeing all his delicious skin and abs carved from granite, heat instantly pools between my legs.

When I move closer, Noah's head turns to me. Immediately the controlling look darkens his eyes as he leans back against the tiles.

I step under the spray of warm water, and with my gaze locked on his, I sink down to my knees.

NOAH

Carla's been tired the whole week, and her appetite is almost non-existent. I'm really starting to get worried. I've made sure she gets eight hours of sleep a night, but it hasn't changed anything.

Googling for reasons, I go through the list.

Chronic fatigue syndrome. Nope.

Pregnancy. Carla's on the pill, but there's always the possibility.

I keep scanning down the list.

Flu. Nope.

PMS. We've had sex, so I definitely would've known.

A frown begins to form between my brows, and then my eyes lift to Carla's.

Shit, could she be pregnant?

I wait for her to finish her coffee, then ask, "When is your period due?"

Her eyebrows pop up. "Not a question I expected first thing in the morning."

I tilt my head. "When?"

"In two days. Why?"

I shake my head. "No reason." *Yet.*

If she misses her period, then I'll get pregnancy tests so we can check if that's the cause for her not feeling well.

She hides a yawn behind her hand as she picks up the coffee pot. I reach for the coffee to stop her from having another cup, saying, "I'd rather you have some electrolytes. It's healthier."

I dissolve a tablet for her and make sure she drinks it all.

When we're ready, I pick up her bag, and taking hold of her hand, we walk out of the suite.

"All the work has probably just caught up with me," Carla says as we step inside the elevator.

"Yeah," I agree.

Carla's been attending Trinity for almost six weeks. She should've adjusted by now.

My gut knows the reason already, but my mind's not so sure.

——————————

I've purchased a pack which contains three tests, just to be sure of the result. The box says it can give an accurate result six days before a period is due, so we should know the outcome today.

Walking into Carla's room, I lock the door behind me before I move to the side of the bed. Sitting down, I stare at her sleeping face.

No matter the outcome, I'll be here for her.

I feel a twinge of panic, not because our future might change in a couple of minutes, but because I'm not sure how Carla's going to handle the news.

Leaning over her, I press a kiss to her forehead, then to her cheek, and finally to her lips. Pulling back, I murmur, "Time to get up."

Carla turns onto her back and stretches.

My gaze drops to her exposed stomach, and lifting my hand, I brush my fingers over her warm skin.

There's a foreign sensation in my chest. Something akin to an ache... wanting more... wanting it all with Carla.

When her gaze settles on mine, I murmur, "Sit up."

She scoots up against the pillows. I reach for her hand and fold my fingers over hers.

Facing the situation head-on, I say, "Your period is late." I know this because I was deep inside her last night. "I got a box with three pregnancy tests."

Carla's eyes widen, and then a frown forms. "I'm probably just late from the stress."

"I still want you to take them." I bring up the box from where I kept them hidden next to me. "Please."

The moment Carla's gaze locks on it, anxiety blooms over her face.

Lifting my hand, I frame her cheek. "Look at me." Her eyes dart to mine. "We're going to be fine, whatever the outcome."

Carla swallows hard before she scoots off the bed. I walk to the bathroom with her and place the box on the counter. Taking hold of her jaw, I press a kiss to her lips, then say, "Let me know when you're done."

As I leave and pull the door shut behind me, my last view is of Carla staring at the box as if it's a death sentence. I almost cave and go back in, but knowing she needs privacy, I go sit on the edge of the bed.

Ten minutes pass excruciatingly slowly, and I'm just about to knock on the door when it opens.

Carla looks pale as she steps aside. "It says we have to wait three minutes."

Taking hold of her arm, I pull her back into the bathroom with me. Carla turns her back to the three tests, hiding her face against my chest. She wraps her arms around my waist. My eyes stay glued to where the lines will appear while I hold Carla tightly.

As the seconds tick by, I begin to hear my heart beating, and my grip on Carla tightens.

The lines begin to appear, faint at first, but they quickly darken on all three tests. I take a deep breath before I pull a little back from Carla. When I frame her face, her eyes dart to mine.

Not wasting time, I say, "You're pregnant." Only then does it settle in my chest, and I feel a burst of unexpected happiness. The corner of my mouth lifts, "We're going to have a child."

Carla's lips part as a sharp burst of air explodes from her. She begins to shake her head, her face paling, then she begins to ramble, "I didn't plan this. I promise." A sob escapes her. "God, my dad's going to kill us. We're dead."

I lean down to catch her eyes. "We're going to be fine. The flu you had probably affected the pill. I should've known that."

Tears begin to gather in her eyes, making them shine like ember stones.

"As for your father, I'll deal with him. Don't worry about it."

Carla nods but then shakes her head again. "You don't know him like I do. He's going to lose his shit."

"I can handle it," I reassure her. I pull her back to my chest and press kisses to her hair while she clings to me as the news sinks in. My lips curve up again. "You're carrying my child. It's earlier than I would've liked, but nonetheless, I'm happy."

Carla pulls back, her eyes snapping up to mine. "Happy?" She sucks in a trembling breath. "You're happy?"

She turns to the tests and her gaze darts over them. "I'm eighteen, Noah. I still have four years of school ahead of me. How am I going to do this?" Her hands lift to cover her mouth. "God, I'm going to be a single mother at eighteen… nineteen. My parents. The media. The other students…" She covers her face as a sob shudders through her.

Standing behind her, I wrap my arms around her. "You're not a single mother. We have nine months to get ready. This isn't going to happen overnight. Don't worry about everyone else. We have a couple of months before you'll start to show. After that, we'll handle one hurdle at a time. Okay?"

Carla turns in my arms as she wipes tears from her cheeks. "How can you be so calm?"

I give her a reassuring smile. "My panicking will not help the situation. Besides, it's not the worst thing that could've happened. I'd much rather you be pregnant than seriously ill."

A look of awe washes over her features as she stares at me, and then she whispers, "You really love me."

My mouth curves up. "Of course. You being pregnant doesn't change how I feel about you."

She shakes her head. "No, it's…" she sucks in a breath of air, "deep down, I couldn't believe you actually loved me… until now." An endearing expression settles in her eyes as she lifts her hand to my jaw. "Most guys would run as fast as they can, but you… are you even real?" A frown mars her forehead again. "Maybe I'm dreaming?"

I let out a burst of laughter and wrap her tightly against my chest. "Nope, this is happening." Framing her face, I press a tender kiss to her lips. "We've created a life together, Carla."

The news only seems to take root now because her face crumbles as she takes refuge against me.

I hold her until she's calmer, and using my thumbs to wipe the tears from her cheeks, I say, "I love you more than anything. I'll take good care of you and our baby."

Chapter 17

CARLA

Standing in the shower, I stare down at my flat stomach.

A million thoughts race through my mind.

Dad's going to be so angry.

Mom might be okay. After all, she was nineteen when she had Jase.

Oh. My. God.

I'm pregnant.

A baby is growing inside me.

I don't feel pregnant, though.

How can Noah be so calm?

I'm going to look like a beached whale in eight months.

I wonder if it's a boy or a girl.

Holy shit.

I'm pregnant.

What will our friends and family think?

Noah's parents?

A knock at the door yanks me out of the mess in my head.

"Carla? Are you okay?" Noah asks. He opens the door and comes into the bathroom, and all I can do is nod.

My nerves are stretched thin, and my stomach feels like it's stuck on spin cycle.

Noah must see the panic on my face because he grabs a towel and turns off the water before he wraps the fluffy fabric around me. Then he slips an arm beneath my knees and my back, and he lifts me to his chest as if I weigh nothing. Feeling the strength in his arms gives me a sense of comfort.

Noah's strong. He's practical and smart as hell. He'll figure out a way for us to get through this.

He goes to sit on the bed with me on his lap and holds me while his mouth brushes over my forehead. "Let's talk about your worries."

"Our parents," I mutter.

"I'll handle them," he assures me.

"We're so young," I voice my next concern.

"We'll adapt. We have time."

"Our friends?"

"They'll support us. You know they will," Noah murmurs.

"Will we stay here?" I wrap my arms around Noah's neck and stare into his eyes, needing to draw strength from him.

"Definitely not." A loving smile tugs at his lips. "We'll get a place of our own."

Emotion wells in my chest, and I lean forward, burying my face in his neck. "You want to live with me?"

"Of course," he murmurs. "There's no way I'm letting you go through a day of this pregnancy, or when our child is born, by yourself. I'll be there every step of the way."

I pull back again and can't keep a tear from falling down my cheek as I look at him. "Are you really okay with this?"

Noah's eyes caress my face, filling me with warmth, and calming my nerves.

"Like I said, it's sooner than I would've liked, but it happened. Whether it's now or in ten years, I'm happy for any life I get to create with you."

Hugging him, I grumble, "I'm going to get fat."

He lets out a chuckle. "You'll still be beautiful."

"What if I'm craving something ridiculous like…" I try to think of the worst possible thing, then continue, "dirt."

Noah begins to laugh. "Then I'll up your iron intake and order you a salad."

My head darts back so I can see his face again. "You've already read everything about being pregnant, haven't you?"

He nods. "Yeah, so get dressed because it's time for you to take your prenatal vitamins." Noah helps me to my feet, then says, "We'll keep the vitamins in your bathroom so the others won't stumble across them."

"Okay." I watch as he picks up a bag he left on the other side of the bed, and as he goes to the bathroom, I turn to my walk-in closet to get dressed. I drag on a pair of jeans and grab a white blouse.

When I'm done, I walk to Noah and can't help but grin when I see the vitamins he wants me to take. Without any argument, I swallow them down before I press a kiss to his cheek. "Thank you for taking care of me."

Noah lifts a hand to my cheek and lightly brushes his knuckles over my skin. "I take my responsibilities seriously."

"Trust me, I've noticed," I tease, then I add, "And I really appreciate it."

"You're welcome." Noah leans in for a kiss, then he murmurs, "I'm going to get dressed so we can have breakfast before classes start."

"Okay." I watch him leave, then start with my makeup and taming my hair into loose curls.

When Noah and I are both ready and we leave the dorm, I'm constantly aware of the fact that I'm pregnant. As if it's something that will show on my face, I keep glancing at the students passing us by, expecting one of them to notice.

Taking a seat at our table, Noah asks, "Is there anything you're in the mood for?"

"Just a bagel with cream cheese and some coffee," I say.

"Remember to only have decaf from now on," Noah reminds me.

I scrunch my nose at him before mumbling, "There goes my caffeine."

Noah reaches for my hand and gives it a squeeze. When the waiter comes, Noah orders two bagels and two decaf coffees.

A wide smile spreads over my face, and the second the waiter leaves, I lean in to kiss Noah. He's always been the man of my dreams, but I never could've imagined how supportive he'd be.

Even though I'm pregnant, deep in my heart, I know I'll be okay as long as I have Noah by my side.

NOAH

When we're done with our classes for the day, I take hold of Carla's hand and pull her toward the parking area.

"Where are we going?" she asks as I open the passenger door for her.

"It's a surprise," I say. I pull the seatbelt over Carla and ensure the lap belt is over her hips and not over her stomach.

I arrange the shoulder strap between her breasts before I lean closer for a kiss.

I shut the door, and once I slide behind the steering wheel, Carla turns her head to me, a loving expression softening her features. "Damn, I've got good taste."

I let out a chuckle. "What are you talking about?"

"My taste in men. I knew you'd be the best, but even my wildest imagination was no match for how amazing you are."

I lean back against the seat and stare at her. "I hope I never do anything to disappoint you."

"You won't," she whispers. When I start the engine, she asks again, "Soooo… where are we going?"

"It's still a surprise," I tease her as I steer the car off campus.

When we drive into town, and I park outside a baby store, Carla's eyes widen. "Seriously? You don't think it's a little early?"

"Nope." I climb out of the car and walk around the front. Opening Carla's door, I say, "Come on."

She gives me a disgruntled look but still takes my hand and climbs out. Once I've locked the car, I link our fingers and pull her into the store. We're instantly submerged in a world of all things babies.

"Oh my gosh, Noah! Look," Carla squeals, and then I'm yanked toward a row of booties. "They're so cute."

I let out a chuckle as Carla pulls me through the store, and I let her fuss over all the tiny clothes.

When we get to the maternity section, I force her to a stop. "This is why we're here." I pick up a bottle of stretch mark prevention cream and read the label. Once I'm satisfied, I hand it to Carla.

She stops in front of something and tilts her head. "What am I looking at?"

I read the box then begin to chuckle. "A pelvic trainer. You won't need it. I'll make sure your pelvis gets all the training it needs."

She lets out a loud snort then covers her mouth.

I get more supplements for her before we stroll through the rest of the store. Carla gets stuck in an aisle filled with stuffed animals, and when she stares at an elephant for a while, I take it from her.

As I lead her to the counter so we can pay, Carla asks, "Are you getting the elephant?"

"Yeah," I set everything down, then place my arm around her.

When I'm done paying, I grab the bag, and linking my fingers with Carla's, we walk back to the car. Once we're inside the cab, I say, "I thought we could come here once a week. Like a baby date?"

Carla grins at me, her eyes sparkling with emotion. "I don't think you'll ever know how much I love you."

I lean over the console and press a kiss to her mouth, then I pull the seatbelt over her. "Gotta keep my baby and my woman safe."

The trip to the store worked like I hoped it would. Carla seems more relaxed as I drive us back to Trinity.

Once we're back in the suite, I carry the bag to Carla's room. I place the supplements with the other vitamins, and I position the stuffed animal against her pillows. When I set the stretch mark cream on the bedside table, I say, "That's for later. I'm going to shower before we go for dinner."

"Can we order in?" Carla asks.

I notice a nervous flutter on her face, and moving closer to her, I tilt my head. "Is there a reason why you don't want to eat at the restaurant?"

She shrugs and lifting a hand, she begins to fidget with the hem of my shirt, then she mumbles, "It feels like the other students can see the word pregnancy written all over my face."

I raise a hand, and placing a finger beneath her chin, I nudge her face up so she'll look at me. "Even if they could, and when they find out, it doesn't matter. What matters is you, me, and our baby. Nothing else."

A heartrending expression makes Carla more beautiful than she's ever been. "Noah…" she breathes, "the three of us sounds like a family."

My mouth curves up. "Yeah."

Her chin begins to tremble. "I never thought I'd get to have a family with you."

I press a soft kiss to her quivering lips, and placing my hand over her stomach, I murmur, "Mine."

Chapter 18

CARLA

As I throw the covers on my bed back, Noah comes into my bedroom. I notice how he locks the door behind him before he moves closer to me.

His eyes drift over my shorts and t-shirt, and then his lips curve up as he murmurs, "You're a little overdressed."

"Yeah?"

Noah takes hold of my shirt and pulls it over my head. I push my shorts down my legs and kick them to the side.

His gaze drops to my panties, and then his eyes flick back up to mine. "Everything."

I can't keep the wide smile from spreading over my face as I step out of my underwear.

I drop my voice low as I ask, "Now that you have me all naked, what are you planning to do with me?"

Noah tips his head at the bed. "Lie down on your back."

I do as he says, but then he reaches for the stretch mark lotion, and I let out a burst of laughter. "Ooooh... am I getting a massage?"

A sexy smirk tugs at Noah's lips as he positions himself between my knees. He takes off his shirt, giving me a perfect view of his chest, abs, and those hot as hell muscles disappearing into his sweatpants. Squirting some lotion into his palm, he warms it before his hands settle on my sides.

My gaze follows his movements as he works his way up to my breasts, every now and then, adding more lotion. When his hands slip down to my thighs, my eyes drift to his face.

It's been a month since Noah kissed me for the first time, and I still marvel at the thought that my dream came true.

He's mine. I'm carrying his child.

Everything happened so fast I don't think it will start to sink in any time soon.

Noah must've noticed that my mind drifted because his palm cups me between my legs, and he pushes a finger inside me.

My eyes focus on his face, and seeing the dominance burning in his hazel gaze makes me part my legs wider for him. He massages me lightly until need begins to pour into my veins.

Then he surprises me by pulling his hand away from me and saying, "Turn on your stomach."

I turn over, and before I can start wondering what he's up to, his hands spread lotion over my back. My eyes drift shut as I let out a moan, murmuring, "Heavenly."

I'm a second away from falling asleep when Noah's hand slips between my legs, and he begins to rub me hard. My head clears of all sleep, and soon he has me grinding back against him. I can feel the orgasm building, but then Noah stops, drawing a frustrated groan from me.

Glancing over my shoulder, I watch as he steps out of his sweatpants, and then he lies down beside me. He pulls me onto my side, and, pushing my legs apart with his own, he positions himself at my entrance.

Entering me with a hard thrust, Noah's mouth latches onto my neck. He pushes his right arm under my head, wrapping it around me, while his left hand finds my clit.

His thrusts grow hard and deep, and each one feels as if he's trying to permanently brand me. Having him seize my body in such a controlling way makes me spiral into a state of bliss.

Just when I think it can't get any better, Noah's thrusts speed up, and the friction sets my body on fire as pleasure shudders through me. It's more intense than I'm used to, and I can only manage silent gasps.

He keeps filling me with fast and hard thrusts, prolonging my orgasm until my body feels sated. Only then does he tense against me, his teeth sinking into my shoulder.

Noah holds me tightly as he catches his breath, and then he says, "That position worked pretty well."

"Definitely," I agree.

His hand moves to my stomach, as he explains, "For when our baby bump starts to grow."

A smile stretches over my face. "Yeah? Are you planning on having sex until I go into labor?"

Noah pulls out of me and turns me onto my back. His gaze is intense as it locks with mine. "Definitely."

"Even when I'm the size of a baby whale?" I tease him.

His mouth curves up. "Don't worry about the weight you'll pick up. Okay? I'm still going to want you even when you're moody and telling me to sleep in the corner of the room."

I let out a burst of laughter because he remembers what I did with the pillow whenever he made me angry.

Lifting my hand to his jaw, I brush my fingers over the day-old scruff. "When did you start to realize you liked me?"

A sexy smirk tugs at his lips. "When you cut off my shirt."

"Yeah?" I wag my eyebrows at him. "Was it the kink factor that got to you?"

Noah shakes his head. "It was the way you looked at me." He presses a soft kiss to my lips. "It was also the first time you touched me." Noah's smile grows. "And then there was the fake orgasm. That kind of sealed the deal."

I laugh because I remember that night as if it happened yesterday. "So I didn't imagine the desire in your eyes."

Noah shakes his head. "Nope. You had me hard as steel."

Needing the bathroom, I say, "Be right back." I go to relieve myself, and after I've washed my hands, my eyes dart to the mirror. For the first time, I don't only feel apprehension as I look at my stomach. My fingers brush over the toned skin, and my mouth curves up at the flutter of excitement.

NOAH

It's been two weeks since we found out we're expecting. Carla's fatigue is much better, and her appetite is normal.

We're sitting in the living room sharing a pizza for dinner when I mention, "I think we should tell our parents."

Carla's eyes dart to mine as she freezes.

Seeing the worry creep into her eyes, I say, "My mom and dad will be fine."

Carla sets the half-eaten slice down on her plate, then asks, "Won't they think less of me?"

I take the plate out of her hands and place it on the coffee table. Pulling her against my chest, I press a kiss to her temple. "My parents aren't judgemental. You'll see. They'll be supportive." I take hold of Carla's jaw and nudge her face up so she'll look at me. "My mom can recommend an obstetrician because you need to start going for monthly check-ups. Okay?"

Carla stares at me for a moment, and when I give her a comforting smile, she nods. "Okay."

"And we need to tell your parents, Carla. Even if they get upset, they need to know. We can't hide it forever."

She lets out a sigh. "I know. I'm just scared. Every time I call them or they call me, I have a mini nervous breakdown."

"All the more reason to tell them. Once it's out of the way, we can focus on our baby."

Carla nods. "You're right."

Aria and Forest come into the suite with containers of food.

"Hi, guys," Carla says, smiling at them. "We're thinking of watching a movie. Want to join us?"

"Sure," Forest replies.

Aria begins to plate their meals, and the instant the smell fills the air, Carla darts up and runs for her room.

I go after her and reach her in time as she sinks to the floor in front of the toilet. I gather her hair away from her face as her body begins to convulse.

"Is she okay?" Forest asks from a safe distance.

"Yeah. Probably the pizza. Can you shut the door?" I ask, and the moment we're alone, I sit down on the side of the tub, rubbing a hand over Carla's back until she's done.

She leans against my leg, taking deep breaths while I flush the toilet and close the lid.

I help her to her feet so she can brush her teeth, and I make sure she drinks some water before I ask, "Feeling better?"

She takes another deep breath, then says, "I don't know what they're having for dinner, but it smelled awful."

"Let's watch a movie in my room. I'll check what they're having so we'll know what brings on the nausea."

"Okay."

Walking out of Carla's room, I watch her go into mine before heading back to the living room. While I close the pizza box and clean our plates, I notice Forest and Aria are having fried chicken for dinner. I take two juices from the fridge then say, "We're going to head to bed. I think an early night will do Carla good. Night, guys."

"Let us know if she needs anything," Aria offers.

"Thanks." I smile before I go back to Carla.

Walking into my room, I close the door behind me then hand Carla an orange juice. "How do you feel?"

"Still nauseous, but better."

I sit down beside her on the bed, stretching my legs out as I lean back against the pillows. "Fried chicken is a no go for you."

Carla shrugs. "I didn't like it that much to begin with." She takes a couple of sips from her juice before she asks, "What are we watching?"

I stare at her until she asks, "What?"

Shaking my head, I say, "Nothing. I'm just thinking about how thankful I am for you."

She scrunches her nose.

Lifting my hand, I tuck some of her hair behind her ear. "Thank you for carrying our child."

Carla's bottom lip juts out, and then emotion washes over her face. "You're going to make me cry."

When I see she's fighting to keep the tears back, I murmur, "Then cry, babe. You don't have to be strong all the time. That's why you have me."

Carla face plants against my chest, and I quickly remove the juice from her hand and set it down beside me on the bedside table. Wrapping my arms around her, I place a hand behind her head and hold her to me.

After a couple of seconds, she mumbles, "I don't even know why I'm crying."

"It's probably your hormones," I explain. "Progesterone, estrogen, and hCG. They say a woman will produce more estrogen during one pregnancy than throughout her entire life when not pregnant."

"Noah," Carla mutters. "No biology lessons. Just hold me."

I let out a chuckle as I press a kiss to her hair. "Okay."

Chapter 19

CARLA

We've decided to tell my parents first, and as Noah steers the car up the driveway, it feels like I'm going to be sick.

"I'm going to throw up," I mutter. Noah brings the car to a sudden stop, and his eyes snap to me. Letting out a chuckle, I add, "From nerves, not because of morning sickness."

"Oh," Noah lets out a sigh of relief. "It would suck if that's the way they find out."

I let out another chuckle. "Yeah, me running into the house to throw up."

Noah gives my thigh a squeeze. "Are you ready?"

"No thanks, I choose life," I impersonate *Sid*.

He lets out a chuckle, then says, "Let's do this."

When we climb out of the car, I rub my hands over my dress to get rid of the sweaty feel.

Yep, today's the day I die.

I take a deep breath as Noah comes to link his fingers with mine, and then we walk to the front door. I let us in with my set of keys, then call out, "We're here."

Mom comes out of the kitchen, a wide smile on her face. "Ahh… finally. I've been telling Carla to bring you over for dinner since she told me you're dating."

Mom gives me a hug before hugging Noah. Besides Mom just wanting me to be happy, she also grew up with Noah's parents, so she's close with them. Which helps a lot. She'll stop Dad from killing us.

"Hi, Sweetheart," Dad says as he comes out of the living room.

My stomach instantly begins to churn with nerves as I lean in to hug him. "Hi, Daddy."

"Noah, welcome. It's good to see you," Dad says as he shakes Noah's hand. "Let's sit in the living room."

We all follow Dad inside, and once we're seated, my leg begins to jump at the speed of light. Noah places his hand over my knee to stop the movement, but it's too late because my parents already noticed.

Dad's eyes dart between us while Mom tilts her head.

Then Mom's eyes widen, and she lets out a gasp. "Oh, my God. You're pregnant."

I pull an 'I'm sorry' face.

Dad's eyes narrow on Noah, and it has me rambling, "I had the flu. I'm sorry."

"What?" Dad grumbles.

"I had the flu, and I think that's why the pill didn't work," I explain.

Dad shakes his head. "So you are pregnant?"

Oh, shit.

I nod, bracing myself for the worst.

Dad just stares at me while Mom darts to her feet, saying, "You're pregnant. Okay." She takes a deep breath. "You're pregnant."

A dark frown forms on Dad's brow as his eyes snap to Noah. "You got my daughter pregnant? Ever heard of a condom?"

"That was a mistake on my part, Sir," Noah replies.

"We both made a mistake, Dad," I jump in, not willing to let Noah take the fall by himself.

"Holy cow," Mom murmurs.

"You fucking impregnated my daughter. She's only eighteen!" Dad growls.

"Yes, the timing isn't ideal. If it were up to us, we would've waited, but seeing as it's happened, I am taking full responsibility," Noah says, still way too calm for how much danger we're in right now.

194

"You bet your ass you'll take responsibility," Dad almost roars. I shrink against Noah's side and grab hold of his hand as emotion pushes up my throat.

God, I knew it was going to be bad.

Noah pulls his hand free from beneath mine, and then he wraps his arm around my shoulders.

The action makes Dad take a moment to breathe through his anger. "Christ," he mutters as he lifts both his hands to rub over his face.

"Calm down, Julian," Mom finally jumps in. "You had me pregnant at nineteen." Dad turns a glare to Mom, which earns him a look a warning from her. "Accidents happen. Biting their heads off won't make it any better."

Mom turns her attention back to me. "How do you feel?"

My chin begins to quiver. "Emotional... happy... scared."

Noah tightens his arm around me, and placing his other hand over mine, he gives me a squeeze for encouragement.

Mom's gaze turns to Noah. "And you, Noah? How do you feel?"

"Like I said, we didn't plan for it to happen, but I'm happy. Carla's an amazing woman, and I'm lucky to have her. I'll take good care of her and our baby."

"When are you getting married?" Dad suddenly asks, making me jump in my seat.

"Seriously?" Mom gives Dad an incredulous look. "They don't have to get married right away."

"I want Carla to have the wedding of her dreams, so we'll get married when she has time to focus on the preparations," Noah answers. "Right now, I'm helping her with her school work, and we're focusing on keeping her healthy."

"My average has gone up since Noah's been helping me," I add. "Noah makes sure I'm taking all my prenatal supplements, and… he's really been amazing."

Dad tilts his head. "So you will finish your MBA even though you're pregnant?"

"Yes."

"We obviously won't live on campus after the baby's born," Noah adds.

His comment makes Dad's eyebrow pop up. "Oh, yeah? Where do you plan on living?"

"We'll get a house of our own," Noah answers.

"Which, I guess, either your parents or we will have to provide?" Dad asks, his eyes narrowing again.

Noah shakes his head, and it has a slight frown forming on my brow because I don't know how we'll afford a house otherwise.

"I've been working every summer since I turned eighteen, and I invested whatever I made. I'm also accelerating my studies, and I'll write my finals in a month so I can start working sooner. I'll be able to take care of Carla without any help from my parents."

Holy shit.

My mouth drops open, and I can only stare at Noah like a gaping fish out of water.

NOAH

The hostility begins to drain from Mr. Reyes' face, which I'm taking as a good sign.

I can feel Carla's eyes on me, but I keep my gaze locked with Mr. Reyes'.

He takes a deep breath, then mutters, "Well, at least you're able to provide for Carla."

"And the baby," Mrs. Reyes adds. She walks over to us, and Carla quickly climbs to her feet. The women hug, then Mrs. Reyes says, "As long as you're happy, I'm happy."

"It's going to take me a while before I'm happy with any of this," Mr. Reyes grumbles, but he still gets up to hug Carla. "God, I can't believe my baby is going to have a baby."

"I'm happy, Daddy," Carla murmurs, and then her shoulders jerk as she buries her face against her father's chest.

It takes every ounce of strength for me to sit still and not to get up and pull her to me.

Mr. Reyes rubs a hand over her back. "It's going to be okay."

Carla pulls back, and when she looks up at her dad with a pleading face and tears on her cheeks, I have to clench my fists against my thighs to keep from moving.

"But you're angry," she whimpers.

Mr. Reyes' expression instantly changes from stern to loving. "No, sweetheart. I'm just shocked. Like your mom said, as long as you're happy, we're happy," he tries to pacify her.

If she ever looks at me like that, I'm in deep shit.

When everyone seems to have calmed down, Mrs. Reyes asks, "Do you know how far along you are?"

"Six weeks," I answer. "Give or take. We still need to confirm the due date."

"How're the symptoms?" Mrs. Reyes asks.

"I can't stand the smell of fried chicken," Carla says.

"Ugh, I had the same," Mrs. Reyes replies.

Mr. Reyes lets go of Carla, and then his gaze locks on me. "Let's leave the women to talk."

I rise to my feet and give Carla a reassuring smile before following Mr. Reyes to his office.

When he shuts the door behind us, he says, "Take a seat."

I wait for him to sit down before I do the same.

Mr. Reyes stares at me for a while, but I meet his gaze, ready for anything. Finally, he asks, "How long have you and Carla been dating?"

"Two months."

He begins to nod slowly while muttering, "Didn't waste any time, did you?"

"I wanted to wait, but then it just happened," I try my best to explain.

"Do you have any intention of marrying my daughter?"

"Yes, but if I propose now, Carla will think it's only because she's pregnant."

He nods again. "True." He tilts his head, lifting an eyebrow at me.

"I do plan on marrying her once our baby is born."

Mr. Reyes lets out a chuckle that sounds more like a warning. His eyes settle hard on mine. "Carla is and always will be my little girl. God help you if you hurt her in any way."

"I won't," I assure him.

He lets out a scoffing sound. "You did once before, so I guess that remains to be seen."

I take a deep breath, then say, "Carla was fifteen. I thought you would understand why I rejected her back then?" I don't wait for his reply but carry on, "I've always wanted the best for her, and I did what was right. I will always do what's right when it comes to her. I love Carla. I've never felt about anyone the way I feel about her."

The corner of Mr. Reyes' mouth lifts slightly, and then he agrees with me, "Yeah, you did the right thing." He leans back in his chair. "So you've been dabbling in investments?"

Knowing the worst is over with, my body relaxes as we begin to talk business.

Tomorrow we'll tell my parents, and then Carla and I can focus on our baby.

Chapter 20

CARLA

Sitting in Mrs. West's office, my knee keeps bouncing until Noah places his hand on my leg. I'm going to have a total nervous breakdown before we're done telling everyone.

I glance at the family portraits on the desk's side and the achievements framed on the wall. My gaze darts to Noah, and I scowl when I see how calm he looks.

"Are you really not worried?" I ask.

"Nope." He even lets that damn 'P' pop, which earns him a glare from me.

Just then, the door opens, and the second I lay eyes on Noah's parents, my heart races out of the office, and I shrink back against the chair.

God. They're going to kill us, and we barely survived my parents.

Noah gets up to give his mom a hug and to shake hands with his father. I force myself to stand on shaky legs.

I manage a nervous smile as I step forward to shake their hands. "Hi, Mr. and Mrs. West. How are you?" At least it doesn't sound like I'm about to have a breakdown.

"Hi, Carla," Mrs. West smiles at both of us as she takes a seat behind her desk.

Imma gonna die.

Mr. West's gaze darts between us, then he asks, "You said you had something to tell us?"

My mouth dries up, and I begin to sweat as if I just ran a marathon. My leg's back to bouncing as if it's trying to break a record.

"Carla's pregnant," Noah drops the nuclear missile.

My eyes widen, and my mouth drops open. I manage to gather myself enough to glare at Noah. "Seriously? That's how you tell your parents?" I turn an apologetic expression to Mr. and Mrs. West. "I'm so sorry. It was an accident. We didn't plan it. I had –"

Mrs. West's mouth curves up in a smile as she interrupts me. "Take a breath, Carla. It's okay."

Either Mrs. West is super good at keeping her composure, or… I don't know. I'm expecting an outburst at any moment.

"Hold up," Mr. West murmurs, and my gaze locks on his face. "Run that past me again."

"Carla's pregnant, Dad. We're having a baby," Noah tells him again.

Mr. West's eyebrows rise as he asks, "How did that happen?"

"Really, Jaxson?" Mrs. West chuckles. "You know how it happened."

My heart's pounding against my ribs, and I clasp my hands tightly together on my lap as my eyes dart between them.

"Yeah," Mr. West mutters. I watch as he takes a deep breath, then he says, "How do you both feel?"

"Happy," Noah answers.

Mr. West's eyes lock with mine, and it has me sputtering, "Like I'm about to have an anxiety attack."

My reaction makes Mr. West smile, and it sets me a bit at ease.

"It's a huge responsibility, but hopefully, it will be a happy one," Mrs. West says.

"It's going to be tough," Mr. West adds. "But as long as you're happy."

Mrs. West seems just as calm as Noah, and then her eyes lock on mine. "Have you had a blood test done?"

I shake my head.

"We'll do one before you leave. Have you seen a gynecologist?"

I shake my head again.

"The hospital has a good doctor. I'll arrange an appointment with her on your behalf." Then she gets up, which also has me rising to my feet, but she indicates that I should sit again. "I'm just going to draw a vial of blood."

"Wow," Mr. West murmurs again, drawing my attention back to him. His gaze keeps darting between Noah and me. "I'm going to be a grandfather."

Mrs. West gets everything she'll need to draw blood and pauses as a smile spreads over her face. "Aww... our first grandbaby."

Noah places his hand over mine. "Relax. I told you my parents would be okay."

God help me.

My eyes almost roll back in my head as I widen them at Noah.

"Of course, it's a shock with you both still at Trinity, but we have to make the best of the situation," Mrs. West says as she pulls a chair closer to my left. She takes hold of my arm and wipes alcohol over the inside of my elbow.

"I'm taking my finals in a month," Noah drops another bomb.

"Yeah, I guess with the pregnancy, that would be the best thing to do," his mother agrees.

"Oh?" Mr. West's eyebrows lift again. "So you're going to start working in the new year?"

Noah nods.

I lean a little closer to Mrs. West and ask, "So you're really not upset?"

She shakes her head, then gently sticks the needle into my arm. I watch as she draws two vials of blood. "You're the ones who will be changing the diapers and getting up at ungodly hours." When she's done, she presses a piece of cotton ball to the site, and meeting my eyes, she continues, "There's no sense in getting upset. We just have to move forward and take it one day at a time. Right?"

"Right," I murmur.

"How far along do you think you are?" Mrs. West asks.

"Give or take, six weeks," Noah answers.

Mrs. West labels the vials then says, "I'll call the moment we have the results."

Noah rises to his feet, so I do the same.

Mrs. West surprises me by coming to give me a hug. Then she murmurs, "Don't hesitate to call me if you need anything."

"Thank you," I reply as she pulls back. Wanting to gain some ground with Noah's parents, I say, "Noah's been great, though."

She gives us both a warm smile and presses a kiss to Noah's cheek. "I have surgery to prep for, but we should have dinner together soon."

"Yes, definitely," Mr. West confirms as he comes to give me a hug before shaking Noah's hand. "Take good care of Carla."

"Of course," Noah answers. "Let me know when's a good time for you, then we'll come over for dinner."

When we leave the office, I frown up at Noah. "That went well, right?"

He lets out a burst of laughter before pulling me into a hug. "Will you relax now? My parents are fine with the pregnancy."

I tilt my head back to meet his eyes. "We survived."

Noah presses a kiss to my mouth, then murmurs, "I never had any doubt that we would."

NOAH

"I'm going to wet myself," Carla grumbles under her breath as we sit in the waiting room to see Dr. Wells. "Why do they tell you to come with a full bladder if they're going to make you wait forever?"

I give her hand a squeeze. "Can you hold for ten more minutes?"

She slants a glare at me. "That's what you asked ten minutes ago. I swear you'll clean up the mess if I pee myself."

"Miss Reyes," the receptionist finally calls. "Dr. Wells will see you now."

"Finally," she mutters while a smile spreads over her face.

When we enter the office, Dr. Wells smiles at us. "Miss Reyes, Mr. West, it's good to meet you."

She indicates that we take a seat, which has me saying, "She needs to use the bathroom. Can we get the urine test out of the way?"

Carla widens her eyes at me while Dr. Wells lets out a chuckle. "Sure."

Once Carla has relieved herself, she comes to take a seat next to me.

Dr. Wells asks a bunch of questions, and once she has all Carla's information on file, she says, "Come lie down for me so we can check if everything is okay with you and the baby."

Carla positions herself on the bed, and Dr. Wells begins with the regular checks. When the doctor squirts a bit of gel onto Carla's stomach, my excitement level shoots up. I move closer and take hold of Carla's hand as Dr. Wells begins to move the Doppler around in the gel.

"It's still early, but let's see if we get lucky today," Dr. Wells murmurs as she keeps moving the Doppler over Carla's skin.

A heartbeat sounds up, which has Dr. Wells explaining, "That's mommy's heartbeat. Baby's will be a lot faster."

My eyes zero in on the Doppler, and then all of a sudden, a fast heartbeat fills the air.

"Oh my gosh!" Carla exclaims, a wide smile spreading over her face.

A wave of emotion hits me right in the chest as I hear our child's heartbeat for the first time. Leaning down, I press a kiss to Carla's forehead before I listen to the quick beat again.

"That's our baby, Noah," Carla whispers.

Smiling at her, I squeeze her hand tightly, my chest humming with happiness and pride.

Dr. Wells gives Carla a paper towel to wipe up the gel, and then she says, "You're around eight weeks pregnant, which means your baby's the size of a raspberry. Soon all the essential organs and body systems will begin to develop."

My eyes dart to Carla's face, which is filled with rapt wonder.

"At your sixteen-week check-up, we should be able to determine the sex. Will that be something you want to know beforehand?"

Carla's eyes dart to mine as she begins to nod excitedly.

"That would be a yes," I chuckle.

"Good. Make your next appointment at reception on the way out." Dr. Wells rises from her chair and shakes both our hands.

After stopping at reception, we leave the hospital. Carla tightens her grip on my hand and almost begins to bounce next to me. "We have a little raspberry."

A wide smile spreads over my face when I see how happy she is. "A raspberry with a strong heartbeat," I murmur.

Once we're in the car, I drive us to the baby store. "Only one stuffed animal," I warn her as we climb out of the vehicle.

Carla pouts at me. "Fine."

"You already have five. At this rate, there will be no space in your bedroom for anything else if we keep getting one every week."

We walk into the store, and Carla heads straight for the newborn section. "Noah, look!" She grabs something, and then I come face to face with a tiny elephant. "It's an elephant ring rattle, and it will match the first stuffed animal we got."

Wrapping my arm around Carla's shoulders, I pull her tightly to my side and say, "I wish you could see the excitement on your face when we're here."

She grins at me, then she says, "It's because I'm getting a cuteness overload."

Wandering through the store, I make sure to get more stretch mark lotion before heading to the register to pay.

The cashier, Chrissie, recognizes us, and smiling, she asks, "Will that be all for today?"

Carla nods. "Thank you."

"How far along are you?" Chrissie asks.

Carla's hand protectively settles over her stomach as she replies. "Eight weeks."

When we're done paying, Chrissie chuckles, "See you next week."

Leaving the store, Carla chuckles, "We're regulars already."

When we're back in the car, I ask, "When do you want to tell our friends?"

Carla shrugs. "Seeing as our parents know, it doesn't really matter when the rest find out about Raspberry."

"Raspberry," I repeat. "Is that what you're going to call the baby?"

"Yeah, I like it."

Seeing the happy glow on Carla's face, and knowing everything is going well with the pregnancy, fills my heart with more joy than I ever thought I'd experience in a lifetime.

Chapter 21

CARLA

After telling our parents, we figured it's only right we let our siblings know next.

We've asked Dash and Jase to meet us for lunch because we're telling Kao and Fallon tonight.

"I'm starting to get the hang of this," I mutter as we walk into a restaurant near the business district where both Dash and Jase's offices are situated.

"We should've gathered everyone together and done it in one blow," Noah says.

Dash is already waiting at a table, and when she spots us, she gets up to give us each a hug, then she looks at Noah, "It feels like I haven't seen you in ages."

"It's been a while," Noah agrees.

He pulls a chair out for me and waits for me to sit before he takes a seat next to me.

Smiling at Dash, I ask, "How are you?"

"I'm good." She gives us both a knowing look. "You're either getting married, or you're pregnant."

I let out a sputter of laughter. "Pregnant."

"Yeah, I figured as much when you asked Jase and me to meet with you."

Just then, Jase appears at the table, and after greeting everyone, he takes a seat. "What's up?"

"I'm pregnant," I blurt out.

Jase stares at me for a moment, then his eyes slant toward Noah. "This is your way of taking care of my sister?"

"It's not like we planned it," I grumble at Jase. "It happened, and we're happy."

"That doesn't mean I have to be happy about it," Jase snaps. "Christ, Carla, you're eighteen."

"Nineteen in a month"

"Doesn't mean shit. You're too young," Jase argues.

An awkward silence falls over the table.

Noah takes a deep breath and turns his gaze to Jase. "Obviously, we would've liked to wait, but Carla's pregnant, and nothing's going to change that. I'll be there every step of the way."

Jase's eyes snap to me. "What did Dad say?"

"He wasn't happy, but he understands," I answer. Then I give Jase a pleading look. "We can't change what happened. Please, just be happy for me now."

He shakes his head and stares at the table cloth. "How are you going to finish your studies? What about your position at CRC?"

"I'm not going to stop studying. God, you make it sound like my life is over," I mutter, a second away from losing my temper.

"I'm helping her with her school work. She won't fall behind," Noah adds.

"Will you finish sooner, Noah?" Dash asks.

"Yes, I'll start at Indie Ink in January."

Jase's eyes dart back to Noah. "That means you have to write your finals in a month."

Noah shrugs. "I can write them tomorrow."

"At least that will take care of finances," Jase grumbles. He stares at me, and then he lightly shakes his head again. "You're happy? This is what you want?"

I don't hesitate to answer, "More than anything."

Jase signals for a waiter. "I don't care what the time is, I need a drink."

"So you're okay?" I ask.

"Not today, but once I'm over the shock, I'll be fine," Jase mutters.

Dash places her hand on mine. "I'm happy for both of you. If I can help with anything, just let me know."

I let out a sigh as I lean back.

Two down, a hell of a lot still to go.

NOAH

Kao's already standing on the porch as I pull up the driveway.

Damn, I've been so caught up with Carla and the pregnancy, I haven't seen Kao in way too long.

When we reach him, I give him half a hug. "Good to see you."

"You too."

I wait for Kao to hug Carla before we go inside.

Kao and I hang back so Fallon and Carla can have a moment to hug and catch up.

"How's the relationship going?" Kao asks.

"Very well." I take hold of his arm and pull him toward the living room. "Take a moment to brace yourself," I warn him.

His eyes widen. "Why? Are you going to ask her to marry you?"

I shake my head and leaning closer to him, I whisper, "Carla's pregnant." Kao starts to blink as if he's going to malfunction, and it has me repeating, "We're expecting a baby."

Kao nods, his eyebrows shooting into his hairline. "I heard you the first time." He takes a moment to process the words, and then we hear Fallon shriek with excitement.

"I guess Carla just told her."

Kao's eyes lock with mine, then he asks, "Are you happy?"

A smile spreads over my face. "More than words can explain."

He leans in and gives me a tight hug. "Then I'm happy for you."

The women come into the living room, and we instantly pull apart.

Fallon comes to give me a hug, murmuring, "Congrats, Daddy-to-be."

We all take a seat, and then Fallon begins with the questions. "How far along are you?"

Carla smiles brightly as she answers, "Raspberry is eight weeks old."

"Raspberry… ahhhhh." Fallon jumps up to hug Carla again. "I love it."

For a while, Kao and I just sit and listen as Fallon and Carla talk non-stop, then he asks me, "Is it safe to guess that you'll be getting a place of your own now?"

"Yeah, that reminds me. Can I get the contact details for the agent you purchased your house through?"

"Sure." Kao forwards the business card to my phone, then he says, "Wow." He stares at me as if the news only sunk in now. "I'm going to be an uncle."

"I'm going to be an aunt," Fallon exclaims excitedly, then she continues, "Just let me know if you want me to organize the gender reveal party, the baby shower, and help with anything else."

The conversation then turns to the gender reveal party, and it has Kao standing up. "We'll go get something for dinner while the two of you plan the baby's entire life."

Rising to my feet, I press a kiss to Carla's forehead before Kao, and I leave to get food.

As soon as we're in the car, Kao asks, "Who else knows."

I grin at him. "Only our parents, Dash, and Jase."

Instantly a smile spreads over his face. "When are you going to tell the rest of the family and friends?"

I shrug. "We're working our way through the list. We're telling Forest and Aria when we get back to the suite."

"How did it go when you told Carla's parents," he asks.

"It was like walking through a ring of fire," I joke.

Kao lets out a chuckle. "I'm sure she's worth it."

Smiling at Kao, I say, "She is."

"Who would've thought you'd end up with Carla," Kao states, a teasing tone in his voice.

"I never stood a chance," I chuckle. "Like Carla always said, it was only a matter of time."

I let out a sigh as I steer the car into a parking bay. "I'm just glad she never gave up."

"Yeah? A couple of months back, I remember you singing a different tune," Kao teases me.

Chapter 22

CARLA

Only one more week, and then we might find out whether Raspberry's a boy or a girl.

I'm sitting in the library, trying my best to focus on my work, but my mind keeps drifting to Raspberry and how happy Noah and I have been.

We've gone to look at a couple of houses, but none of them were to my taste. We have time, though, so we're not in too much of a rush.

I let out a sigh as I read over the same paragraph for the fourth time.

Now that our families and friends know, I'm don't care about the other students finding out.

I glance at the time and notice I only have an hour left before meeting Noah for dinner.

With my hand resting on my stomach, I force my attention back to my work. With all the help Noah's been giving me, I've been able to up my overall average, but I can't expect him to help me with all my work.

The thought helps me focus, and I manage to get half the assignment done before I have to pack up.

Clearing the table I used, I grab my bag and make my way out of the library.

I take the stairs down, then turn right toward the dorm. Pulling my phone out of my bag, I message Noah.

C: Are you at the restaurant?

It takes a couple of seconds for him to reply.

N: I just left the suite.

My eyes dart up, and I watch as Noah steps out of the dorm. He turns toward the restaurant when there's a loud crash behind me. Glancing over my shoulder, I watch as a car drives through the security barrier.

A gasp explodes over my lips as students pile out of the library to see what the commotion is about.

The car comes to a skidding stop on the stretch of lawn beside the parking area, which is right across from me.

I feel a flutter of relief when the driver stumbles out of the car. He begins to wave something around, yelling, "Where's Noah West?"

A frown forms on my face until it registers what he's holding. The blood drains from my face as my head turns back toward the dorms.

I see Noah staring at the man.

"Noah West!" The man shouts, sounding hysterical. He waves a gun recklessly around as he begins to stumble into the street.

Not thinking, I drop my bag and begin to run toward Noah.

NOAH

Coming out of the dorm, I hear a loud commotion. My head snaps in the direction of the main entrance, in time to see a car driving right through the security barrier.

"What the fuck?" I mutter as I watch the vehicle come to a screeching halt opposite the library.

A man stumbles out, waving a gun at all the students in his near vicinity. "Where's Noah West?" he shouts.

Holy shit.

My heartbeat speeds up uncontrollably as he turns in my direction. I stand frozen with shock as security guards run toward him.

"Noah West!" The man shouts, sounding hysterical. He waves the firearm around as he begins to stumble into the street.

"Noah!" I hear Carla scream. "Run!"

My head snaps toward Carla's voice, and all my breath rushes from my body as she sprints toward me.

No!

I dart forward, shouting, "Get down, Carla!"

There's a panicked look on her face as she runs to me.

My eyes dart to the man, and I watch as a security guard tackles him. A gunshot reverberates in the air as they hit the concrete, and the noise sends ripples of shock racing over my skin.

The guards manage to restrain him and kick the gun out of his reach.

My gaze turns back to Carla, and it takes a split-second for my world to implode. She stumbles to a halt, and her eyes lock on mine before she slumps to her knees.

"No. No. No." I dart forward and drop down in front of her. "No," I breathe, and then she coughs, and blood sprays over my neck and shirt.

Fuck.

God, no!

Everything I've been taught by my mother rushes into my mind as my emotions spiral into a chaotic mess. I move behind her, and seeing the crimson stain growing on her back, I quickly press my hand against the wound to keep air from being sucked in so her lung won't collapse.

My eyes dart around us, and then they lock on a guard that's running toward us. "Get a car! We need to get her to the hospital."

He turns and runs in the direction of where the SUVs are parked.

Gunshot wound to the chest has an eighty percent survival rate.

But our baby?

Carla coughs again, and it makes my gaze snap back to her. Her eyes are locked on my face, and seeing the fear reassures me she's still alert.

"You're going to be fine," I say as I dig my phone out of my pocket and dial my mother's number.

Mom doesn't answer on the first try, so I keep pressing redial until she finally answers, "Noah, what's wrong?"

I ramble all the information she'll need, "Carla's been shot in her back. I think it hit her lung. She's coughing up blood. I have the wound covered with my hand. We're bringing her in. I need you to be ready."

"Okay. I'll get an operating room ready for her. I'll be at the emergency entrance to receive her."

Ninety-five percent survival if we get her to the hospital with her heart still beating.

That's all I have to do. Just keep Carla's heart beating.

The guard kneels next to me, and I quickly shove my phone back in my pocket. We work together to lift Carla into the back of the SUV without moving my hand away from the wound. I get in with her and then press as hard as I can against her back.

The guard speeds us away from campus, and he must've had training because he's doing a damn good job maneuvering the car through any traffic we come across.

Carla coughs again, and it's only then feeling returns to my body. It hits me like a tidal wave. Seeing her struggling to breathe rips my heart right from my chest.

"My mom's waiting for you. You're going to be fine," I begin to reassure her.

Carla manages to grab hold of my thigh, but her grip is weak. "Noah." Her breathing becomes shallow, and when I hear crackling sounds, I quickly lift my hand from the wound. There's a hissing sound as the built-up air escapes, and then I cover the bullet hole again, applying pressure.

Our eyes meet, and Carla struggles to say, "Raspberry."

"You're both going to be fine," I try to reassure her. "We're almost at the hospital."

My heart thunders in my chest as worry for both Carla and our baby grinds against my soul.

I glance out the front window to see where we are and let out a breath of relief when I notice we're almost at the hospital.

The moment we stop in front of the emergency entrance, Mom jogs toward us, and just seeing her offers me a world of relief. She yanks the door open, and I have to move quickly to get out of the way.

I watch as they load Carla onto a stretcher, and an oxygen mask is placed over her nose and mouth. Mom glances at me, and then they're running, wheeling Carla toward the operating room.

I follow them as far as I'm allowed to go, and then I stand, feeling numb to my core.

I don't understand what happened.

Who was that man?

Why did Carla get shot?

Why did any of this happen?

My mind races for answers, but there's none.

The woman I love more than life itself got shot, and I have no idea what that means for our baby.

My eyes drift closed as a helpless feeling settles darkly inside me.

Please, Mom. Please save them both.

Chapter 23

NOAH

My legs lose all strength, and I sink to my knees, my blood-covered hands lying limply on my thighs.

I keep hearing Carla's scream. The gunshot.

I see her stumble before she drops to the ground.

The sound of her coughing.

Her blood splattering over me.

Her eyes.

God, her eyes. She was so scared.

I suck in a breath as the images and sounds play on an endless loop in my mind like a horror movie.

Why?

Why did this happen?

I feel hands on my shoulders, and then I'm pulled up. My sight manages to focus on my father's face.

"She's in the best hands, son," Dad says.

I nod and murmur, "I know."

"Let's get you cleaned up." Dad turns me away from the doors Carla was pushed through and guides me to a restroom. He helps me wash the blood from my hands. Taking a paper towel, Dad wets it, and then he wipes the blood from my neck and jaw.

When he's done cleaning me as best he can under the circumstances, he frames my face and his eyes lock with mine. "Carla and the baby will survive. Okay?"

I shake my head and whisper, "Why?" I suck in a breath of air, and then my body begins to convulse. I dart to the toilet, and dropping to my knees, I empty my stomach.

I feel Dad's hand on my back, and then he hands me a paper towel. I wipe my mouth before I get up. The shock lifts, and in its wake lies the worst pain I've ever felt.

It's sharp, merciless, unfathomable – eating away at my heart.

I press a hand to my chest as I try to breathe through it.

Dad pulls me against his chest and wraps his arms tightly around me. "I've got you, son. It's okay."

There's no comfort in my father's arms. This isn't a scraped knee or a black eye.

This is… this is… excruciating.

"Dad," I groan. "I can't process this. I can't comprehend what happened." I suck in a suffocating breath as I grip him tighter. "It's like an equation I can't solve."

"My boy," he murmurs, his voice tight with pain for me. "This isn't something you can solve. I know it fucking hurts right now, and you're worried out of your mind, but in a couple of hours, you'll see that they're fine. Your mom is the best, and she'll save them."

I'm caught in a maze where nothing makes sense. There's no way out. There won't be any way out of it until I find out why, until I see Carla again and hear that our baby is fine.

Until then, I'm stuck.

I'm frozen in time until Carla returns to me because, without her, there's no tomorrow.

I need to hear her laughter and her sass. I need to see her smile. I need to feel the heat from her body.

During the past three months, she's become... the very meaning of emotion for me. She's love. She's happiness.

Without Carla, there's nothing but cold hard facts.

There's no warmth.

Dad pushes me back, and his worried gaze searches mine. "Your mother will save them both. Okay?"

Another wave of shock and pain hits, and I struggle to take a breath. "Dad," I groan, unable to process the intense heartache ripping my world to shreds.

Dad's arms instantly tighten around me again. "I've got you, my boy. I've got you."

———————————

I'm sitting like a zombie in the waiting room. Dad keeps rubbing a hand over my back.

Suddenly there's a commotion, and the room fills with Carla's family and our friends.

Dad gets up to talk with them, but I can't even manage to lift my head. Someone sits down beside me and pulls me into a hug, then I hear Kao say, "I'm here."

I close my burning eyes, unable to say anything.

I feel a hand on my knee, and when I open my eyes, and I see Fallon, something breaks inside me.

The same silky brown hair.

The same golden-brown eyes.

I see some of Carla's features in her cousin, and right now, it's killing me.

I want my Carla back.

Lifting a hand, I cover my eyes, and the moment Fallon's arms wrap around me, my shoulders shudder.

"Shh…" she whispers. "Carla's strong."

She is. Carla's the strongest person I know. She never backs down from a fight. God, she gave me hell for three years.

The thought rips a gasp from my lips as the wave of heartache washes my world from under my feet.

For three years, I kept her at a distance. I was cold and downright harsh at times.

Then I gave in, and she fucking changed everything. She turned my world on its head. She added a deeper meaning to every single second.

"Can I bring you something to drink?" Fallon asks.

I shake my head because I know I won't be able to stomach anything until I hear Carla and Raspberry are fine.

Raspberry.

My shoulders shudder again under the strain of the distress.

I don't know how much time has passed, but my head snaps up the instant I hear Miss Sebastian say, "The surgery is going well. The bullet has been removed, and Dr. West is now repairing the lung and draining the blood that has built up. It should take another hour before Miss Reyes is moved to the ICU for recovery. Dr. West will see you then." Miss Sebastian looks at me. "The baby's also doing well under the circumstances. Dr. Wells was present during surgery."

I feel a slither of relief trickle through my insides. Kao gives me a supportive squeeze.

Miss Sebastian smiles at me. "I wish I could hug you, my god-baby, but I have to get back. They will be fine. Okay?"

I nod, still unable to form words.

She blows me a kiss before she hurries back to the operating room.

Getting up, I rush to the nearest restroom. The moment I'm inside, and Kao's arms fold around me, I can't keep the tears from coming.

I grab hold of my best friend as I lose all control over my emotions.

I promise I'll be the best husband and father.

My shoulders shudder.

Please give me the chance to be what Carla deserves. Give me a chance to hold our baby.

I just want them safely back in my arms.

Please.

After I manage to regain control of my emotions, Kao and I go back to the waiting room.

I walk to Mr. and Mrs. Reyes, and after shaking Mr. Reyes' hand, I say, "I'm so sorry."

The words sound empty to my own ears.

Mrs. Reyes rises from the chair, and then her arms wrap around me. Getting to hold Carla's mother offers me a sense of comfort I haven't felt since Carla got shot. It's like I'm holding a piece of her.

When Mrs. Reyes pulls back, she places a cool palm to my jaw. "It wasn't your fault. Okay?"

Her words make me frown. "What do you mean?"

Mr. Reyes pats my shoulder, then he explains, "The man who shot Carla lost his son three months ago. Your mother was his son's doctor. After the death of his son, the man suffered a breakdown due to the grief."

My mind rushes to retrieve the information I have on the patient Mom lost.

I have a twenty-year-old male patient who was rushed in with an aneurysm. Basically, the thoracic aorta consists of the aortic root...

My twenty-year-old male patient died. The aorta ruptured, and he bled out within minutes. There was nothing I could do.

234

My eyes lock with Mr. Reyes'. "So he came to Trinity to take revenge?"

Mr. Reyes nods.

The facts sink into my gut like hot coals.

That man was there to kill me, and instead, Carla got shot.

I close my eyes against the realization.

Mrs. Reyes' arms wrap around me again, and on autopilot, I hold her.

I feel a hand on my back, and glancing to my right, I see it's Dad. He smiles at Mr. and Mrs. Reyes, then says, "Carla is in good hands."

———————

When Mom finally walks into the waiting room, I jump to my feet.

Her eyes lock on mine, and she reaches a hand for me. When my fingers wrap around hers, she turns her attention to Mr. and Mrs. Reyes as well. "Carla is in recovery. The surgery went well. She'll be in the ICU until she's able to breathe on her own. I'm confident we'll be able to move her to a private room tomorrow. Dr. Wells is happy with how the baby is doing. It's a waiting game now."

"Thank you, Leigh," Mrs. Reyes says as she comes to hug Mom. "Thank you."

"Of course." Then Mom turns to me, and she wraps her arms around me. After we've hugged, Mom says, "I made several small cuts over the chest wall, and I performed a video-assisted thoracotomy surgery. I felt it would be less invasive. I removed the bullet and drained all the blood that built up. Carla will heal faster than if I'd performed an open lung surgery. She has a chest tube in to drain any fluid that might build up."

I nod to show I understand.

"Carla will probably have to stay in the hospital for five to seven days, depending on how quickly she heals." Mom's eyes lock on Carla's parents. "As she's in the ICU, we can only allow two visitors at a time, but for the first visit, we'll allow both of you and Noah." Mom turns her gaze to me. "But you only get five minutes, then you need to go shower and change into clean clothes."

I nod, just happy I'll get to see Carla.

I let Mr. and Mrs. Reyes walk first before I follow after them. We sanitize our hands and entering the ICU, Mom gestures to our left.

The moment my eyes land on Carla, there's a severe blow to my gut. Seeing all the tubes, the IV, the machines… they make her look so fucking fragile.

Slowly, I move closer as if any sudden movement might hurt her. Mrs. Reyes lets out a soft sob as she takes in the state of the daughter.

Mr. Reyes looks at me. "You go first, Noah."

"Thank you," I murmur as I move to the other side of the bed. I reach for Carla's hand, and the moment my fingers brush over her warm skin, my heart squeezes painfully.

I move my other hand to her stomach and keeping my touch gentle, my eyes drift shut.

They're alive. That's all that matters.

Right now, Carla and Raspberry are still with me.

Leaning over Carla, I press a kiss to her forehead, then I murmur, "Keep fighting for me. I love you." I press another kiss to her skin, then I pull back.

I move to the foot end of the bed, and as Mr. Reyes passes by me, he gives me a smile.

My eyes go back to Carla's face, and I just drink in the sight of her. My emotions keep fluctuating between hope and apprehension.

Mom takes hold of my arm, and leaning into me, she says, "Kao's waiting to take you home. Try not to worry too much. I'll take good care of them."

I press a kiss to her cheek, murmuring, "Thank you, Mom."

As I leave the hospital with Kao, I'm exhausted, but I know there's no way I'll be able to find a moment's rest until I hear Carla's voice and see her eyes again.

Chapter 24

NOAH

When we reach Trinity, I say, "You should be with Fallon. I'm just going to shower and get some sleep."

I can see Kao's torn as he asks, "Are you sure?"

Like Carla's become the most important person in my life, Fallon is that to Kao. "Yeah. I'll call you when I wake up."

Kao stops the car in front of the dorms, and as I open the door, he says, "Call me any time. Okay?"

I meet his eyes for a moment and even manage a weak smile. "Thank you for everything."

"Of course."

I climb out, and after shutting the door, I watch as Kao drives away. I glance over the area between the dorms and the library. There's no sign of the traumatic event which took place this afternoon.

My feet begin to move until I reach the spot where Carla fell. Crouching, my eyes scan for any signs of blood, but there's none. The staff must've cleaned up.

Rising back to my feet, I head to the suite, and the moment I'm standing in the middle of my room, the days' events replay in my mind.

The car crashing through the security barrier.

Carla's scream.

The gunshot.

Carla dropping to the ground.

The sound of her coughing.

Her blood splattering over me.

Her eyes.

Remembering her fear makes me snap. A growl builds in my chest as I lash out at the laptop and stationery on my desk. Angrily, I sow destruction in my room until nothing looks like it used to. I drop to the floor and bite into the back of my hand as the anger turns to a raw ache.

Sucking in a desperate breath, I try to regain control of my chaotic emotions, but unable to, I shout, "Fuck!"

Just then, the door to my bedroom opens, and Kao comes in. He takes one look at me and grumbles, "Yeah, I thought so." He comes to sit next to me. "Fallon is with her family. I'm staying."

I begin to shake my head, which has Kao growling, "I'm staying."

After a couple of seconds, I whisper, "She looked so fragile hooked up to all those machines."

"The surgery went well," Kao reminds me.

"Yeah," I murmur, my voice hoarse from the worry.

CARLA

Waking up, a weird whooshing sound draws my attention, and then it's joined by a beeping sound. It sounds like a car is idling in the distance.

Confused, I blink.

A sharper beep that sounds similar to an alarm gets through the brain-fog.

I hear voices and movement, and then I feel a kiss against my temple.

It takes more strength than I have to pry my eyes open.

"Sweetheart," I hear Dad exclaim.

My sight won't focus on anything but blurs of light.

"Baby, hello... you're doing so well," I hear Mom.

"Ah…" Dad sighs with absolute relief, and I feel another kiss on my forehead. "You're so strong."

"We love you," Mom says before a relieved chuckle escapes her.

Noah.

Raspberry.

My parents fade down a dark tunnel as I can't stay awake any longer.

NOAH

Mom: Carla woke up for a moment. There's no mucus forming in her airways, and she's recovering at a satisfactory rate. Both she and the baby are doing well. Love you.

My body goes lax with relief.

Kao left twenty minutes ago to be with Fallon. I shower quickly and rush through my routine.

Taking a deep breath, I tuck my phone in my pocket as I head to Carla's room. I grab the first stuffed animal we bought for Raspberry from her bed, and then I leave the suite.

When I get to the hospital, I quickly walk to the ICU. I sanitize my hands and then head inside.

Miss Sebastian comes to give me a hug. "They're doing well."

"That's good news." I walk to Carla's bed and smile at Mrs. Reyes. "Where's Mr. Reyes?"

"He went to get some coffee. We can take turns to sit with Carla."

"Thank you."

Setting the elephant down by Carla's feet, I lean over her and press a soft kiss to her forehead. "Hi…" my voice cracks on the word, and I take a deep breath of Carla's scent to calm my emotions.

As I pull back, her eyes open, and the sight of her brown irises sends a rush of goosebumps over my body. "Carla," I gasp, pure relief and joy instantly making me feel high. I grab hold of her hand. "Squeeze my hand if you can hear me." Her grip is weak, but it's there.

Mrs. Reyes presses a kiss to Carla's temple. "I love you, my baby." She gestures for me to continue.

"Raspberry's doing well," I say, and Carla squeezes my hand again. "Keep fighting." A weaker squeeze. "I love you more than anything." Her fingers lose all strength as her eyes drift shut.

I press another kiss to her forehead, and keeping my mouth against her skin, I close my eyes as I soak in the feel of her.

"She keeps waking up for brief moments. It's a good sign," Mrs. Reyes says.

Straightening up, I smile at Carla's mom. "Yeah."

My gaze instantly returns to Carla's face. I stand and stare at the woman who holds my life in the palm of her hand.

"You really love her," Mrs. Reyes says.

My gaze darts to hers. "With all my heart."

A smile spreads across Mrs. Reyes' face. "I'm glad."

I place my other hand on Carla's stomach and murmur, "Daddy's here. Just keep growing. I can't wait to meet you."

Carla's eyes flutter open again, and this time it looks like she's able to focus more.

"Hi, beautiful," Mrs. Reyes coos. "You just keep resting. Okay? You're doing well."

Carla's gaze turns to me, and my lips instantly curve up. "You have another visitor." I pick up the stuffed animal to show her. "He missed you as well."

Leaning over Carla, I press a kiss to the side of her head, and then I say, "I love you. Just keep getting better. I need you."

She squeezes my hand, her grip stronger than before.

With a hand on Carla's stomach and the other holding hers, I stare into her eyes, just taking in the life shining from them.

"Thank you for fighting so hard," I murmur. Her grip feels weaker again, and knowing she'll probably fall asleep soon, I add, "I love you more than anything."

I watch as her eyes drift shut, and then I close my own, sending up a prayer of thanks.

Chapter 25

NOAH

I watch as Mom leans over Carla. "When you cough, the tube will come out. Okay?"

Carla nods.

Mom gets ready, then she smiles at Carla. "Cough for me." I watch as Mom pulls the tube out just as Carla gives a weak cough. "Oh, you did so well," Mom praises her while she positions an oxygen mask over Carla's nose and mouth. Carla coughs twice more, but she seems to be holding her own at the moment.

Mom pats Carla's shoulder as she checks all the vitals. "Let's give it a bit of time, and if you continue to do well on your own, we'll move you to a private room."

Carla nods again.

Mom gives my arm a squeeze, and just then, Mr. and Mrs. Reyes comes back into the ICU. They went home to change into clean clothes.

Mom talks with them, and I take a moment to press a kiss to Carla's temple. "You're badass. I'm so proud of you."

Pulling back, I see Carla's trying to smile. "I'm going to let your parents visit for a while. Okay? Once you're in the private room, I won't leave your side."

Carla nods to show she understands.

I press a kiss to her stomach before I walk to where Mr. and Mrs. Reyes are talking to Mom.

Mrs. Reyes gives me a sideways hug, and then she goes to Carla. "Hi, sweetheart. Are you feeling better?"

I watch as Carla nods, then I leave the ICU.

"Noah," Mom calls behind me. I stop and turn back to her. "Dr. Wells will do a scan as soon as we move Carla to a private room. If she continues to breathe on her own, it will probably be in two hours."

Happiness courses through my veins, and I grab Mom in a hug. "That's the best news. Thank you so much, Mom. God, you're a miracle worker."

Mom lets out a chuckle. "Go have something to eat, please."

"I'll just hang out in the cafeteria while I wait."

"That's a good idea. I'll message you when we're ready to move, Carla."

I press a kiss to Mom's cheek.

When I start to walk down the hallway, Mom says, "Don't have the meatloaf."

I let out a chuckle. "Okay."

I've just taken a seat at a table with a chicken sandwich when Mr. Reyes comes in. He gets himself a coffee before he comes to join me.

We sit in silence for a while, then I mention, "My mom said Dr. Wells will do a scan later. We might be able to determine the sex of the baby. You and Mrs. Reyes should be there."

The corner of Mr. Reyes' mouth tips up. "We'd love that." He takes a sip of his coffee, then his face turns grim as he says, "The man who shot Carla has been admitted to an asylum. They say he suffered a mental breakdown brought on by the loss of his son."

Shaking my head, I mutter, "It's still… I can't believe it happened." My gaze locks with his. "I'm guessing my mother doesn't know yet?"

"No, I thought it would be best if we only tell her after Carla is out of the ICU." He lets out a hollow-sounding chuckle. "Selfish of me, I know. But I wanted her to focus on Carla."

"You did the right thing," I assure him. "I'd like to tell my mom, or she'll blame herself."

"Okay," Mr. Reyes agrees. "Let me know if you want me there."

My mouth curves up. "Thanks, Mr. Reyes."

His gaze meets mine, the corner of his mouth lifting. "You might as well call me Julian, seeing as our lives are intertwined now." Surprised, I stare at him, and it makes him frown as he continues, "Uncle Julian just doesn't sound right."

I let out a chuckle because I can't see myself calling him uncle. "Julian, it is. It might take me a while to get used to calling you by your first name, though."

His smile grows before the serious look returns to his features. "I've watched the security footage on campus." His eyes lock on mine again. "You reacted fast. Thank you."

Unable to accept the thanks, I can only nod because it's my duty to protect Carla. She shouldn't have been shot in the first place.

We both take a deep breath, and after Julian finishes with his beverage, he asks, "Where are you thinking of purchasing a house?"

"We haven't decided on a specific area, and the places we've seen so far weren't to our liking. I got Kao and Fallon's agent's details. I'll give her a call and see what's on the market once Carla has been discharged from the hospital."

"Let me know if you need help," he offers.

My mouth twitches as I suppress the smile.

Carla will be glad to hear things are better between her father and me.

CARLA

For the past two hours, my mind's been racing, trying to catch up with everything that happened. I'm struggling to come to terms with the fact I was shot.

As I'm moved onto the bed in the private room, my parents and Noah stand to the side, so they're out of the way.

Tired, my body relaxes against the pillows.

Miss Sebastian makes sure my IV is flowing right, then she checks my oxygen mask. "There you go. Dr. Wells will come to check on you soon." She points to a remote. "Just press this button if you need assistance."

I nod and say, "Thank you." The words are muted by the mask.

"We'll start decreasing the pain medication, as well," she informs me.

I've only felt discomfort so far, but I'm sure the medication can't be good for Raspberry. "The sooner, the better," I agree, not wanting to risk Raspberry's health.

Miss Sebastian pats my hand before she leaves to attend to her other duties.

Mom's the first to approach the bed. "Is there anything I can bring you?"

I shake my head. "Noah can bring my clothes..." feeling breathless, I take a moment to get air into my lungs, then I continue, "...from the suite."

Dad comes to press a kiss to my forehead, then he says, "I need to get back to work, but I'll see you later. Okay?"

I nod. "Thanks for being here, Daddy."

He gives me a loving smile before he walks back to where Noah is standing.

Noah's eyes meet mine, then he says, "I'm going to pack your bag, then I'll be back."

When the men leave, it's just Mom and me. She takes a seat next to the bed, and her eyes scan over me.

"I'm much better," I say to ease any worry she might have.

Mom nods. "I know." Leaning forward, she takes hold of my hand. "How do you feel emotionally?"

I stare at Mom as I try to gather my thoughts. "I'm confused." I take a couple of breaths. "I don't understand why it happened."

Mom glances at the door before she says, "Noah and your father will talk to Leigh." I frown, the sudden change in topic throwing me for a loop. Then Mom explains, "The shooter's son died during surgery. Leigh was the surgeon. The man blamed her, and he wanted to take revenge by killing Noah."

My eyes widen as I gasp for a breath of air. "What?"

Mom rubs her hand over mine. "He's unstable due to the loss he suffered. Your father watched the footage. When the guards tackled the man, the gun went off, and you got shot. Your Uncle Lake is handling the matter, and he said the man will be in a mental asylum for a very long time. I'm guessing once he's learned to deal with his grief, he'll have to face his guilt as well."

"That's…." I almost say crazy but swallow the word back.

"It's a traumatic event that never should've happened to begin with."

"Yeah," I murmur, thinking I almost lost Raspberry because a man couldn't deal with his grief. "I don't think I'll ever understand it."

Mom presses a kiss to the back of my hand. "You and Raspberry are safe and getting stronger by the second. It's all that matters to me."

"Did Noah tell you…" Damn, I hate that I can't complete a sentence without having to catch my breath, "…that's what I've been calling the baby?"

"I overheard him telling you Raspberry is doing well," Mom explains.

My thoughts turn to Noah. I hope he doesn't blame himself for what happened.

"Try to sleep a bit," Mom murmurs.

Yeah, I don't think that's going to be a possibility until I see Noah.

As if Mom can sense that I'm thinking about him, she says, "Noah really loves you."

Her words make me smile. "I know."

She lets out a chuckle. "He was even talking to the baby while you were in the ICU."

"Yeah? What did he say?"

A soft smile forms around Mom's mouth. "He can't wait to meet Raspberry."

I begin to chuckle, but it turns into a cough.

When my breathing returns to normal, Mom helps me have a few ice chips to ease the dryness in my mouth and throat.

Lying back, I rest my hand on my stomach.

Even though I'm out of the ICU, I'm still worried about Raspberry. I hope the ordeal doesn't affect our baby's development in any way.

Chapter 26

NOAH

Even though Julian offered to be present, I thought it would be best to speak with Mom alone.

Luckily she's able to spare me a couple of minutes, and the moment we're alone in her office, I get right to the point. "Mr. Reyes found out some information about the shooter."

Mom's eyes narrow. "Oh? He's been arrested, right? Have they pressed charges?"

I shake my head. "From what I understand, he's been admitted to an asylum." Mom's frown darkens, which has me explaining. "It's Mr. McKay. His son was your patient a couple of months back."

Shock washes over Mom's features, and it has me reaching for her arm. "The loss of his son led to him suffering a breakdown. He was at Trinity for me, and Carla got caught in the crossfire when the guards tackled him to the ground."

Mom lifts her hands to her face, covering her mouth in disbelief. I pull her into a hug and murmur, "It's not your fault. You did your best to save his son."

Mom shakes her head, and pulling back, she asks, "So he wanted to kill you? He wanted revenge?" Her chin begins to quiver, and I pull her back against me. Rubbing a hand over her back, I say, "I'm okay. Carla and the baby are recovering well."

Mom looks up at me, shaking her head. "But still, Carla got shot because I lost a patient."

"Mom," I say, my tone firmer, "you can't take the blame for someone else's actions. You did your best to save his son. What Mr. McKay did was all on him. Even if he had a mental breakdown, it was still a choice he made."

Mom nods, then she gasps, "I can't believe this happened." Her eyes lock on mine. "I'm so sorry, Noah."

Shaking my head, my face softens. "It wasn't your fault."

Mom nods again. "I need to process it all. I'll talk to Julian and Jamie. God, like it wasn't awful enough, to begin with."

"They don't blame you," I tell Mom. "They know it was an irrational act of violence."

There's a knock at the door. Mom gives me an apologetic look. "I have a patient to see."

"Get back to work. I'm just going to get some things for Carla, then I'll be with her."

"I'll come find you later."

We hug before Mom opens the door, and I quickly leave so she can continue with her work.

Damn, that sucked.

After stopping by the suite and packing a hospital bag for Carla, I rush back to her.

By the time I walk into her room, it feels as if hours have passed, and I'm agitated.

Carla seems to be asleep. I place the bag down on the coffee table in the corner, where a small lounge is set up.

Mrs. Reyes smiles at me and gets up to come check what's in the bag, then she says, "I'm going to get something to eat. Can I bring you something?"

Shaking my head, I say, "No, thanks, Mrs. Reyes."

"You can call me Jamie," she chuckles, then she explains, "Julian said he spoke with you."

The corner of my mouth lifts slightly, then I ask, "How's Carla? Has Dr. Wells been here?"

Jamie shakes her head. "Not yet. Carla's better. She just gets breathless when talking." She begins to walk to the door, then she asks, "Will you call me if Dr. Wells comes while I'm gone?"

"Sure."

When the door shuts quietly behind her, I walk to the side of the bed. Leaning over Carla, I press my mouth to the side of her head, and then I take a deep breath.

The agitation bleeds away, and I instantly feel calmer.

"You're back," Carla suddenly murmurs.

Sitting down on the side of the bed, I brace my right hand beside her head. My eyes lock with hers. "How do you feel?"

"Much better." She lifts her left hand and grips hold of my forearm. "Especially now that you're here."

"Have you sat up yet?" I ask, knowing it's essential for her to start moving around.

When she shakes her head, I slowly help her into a sitting position. Her left hand moves to my shoulder.

I press a kiss to her cheek, then ask, "How's that?"

"Okay," she murmurs.

I position the pillows so Carla can lean against them. "Relax."

She leans back, then she removes the oxygen mask. "My mom told me about the shooter."

My gaze locks on hers, and reaching a hand up, I brush her hair behind her ear. "I'm sorry you got caught in the middle."

Carla shakes her head. "I can't believe he wanted to..." there's a flash of pain on her face, "...hurt you."

"Is sitting up causing you pain?" I ask.

"No, I'm fine," Carla says, her voice stronger. She rests her hand against my jaw. "I'm worried about you. What if he comes after you again?"

Giving her a comforting smile, I say, "He's in an asylum, Carla."

"Yeah, but..."

I shake my head. "Don't worry about it." I lean closer to her and tilt my head. "I won't let something like this happen again. I promise."

"You can't make a promise like that," she argues.

Lifting my hand, I cup her cheek. "It's my duty to protect you. I failed you once. I won't fail you again."

Carla shakes her head, whispering, "Noah."

Before she can continue, I say, "I'm going to get training, so if something like this happens again, I'm ready."

Carla's eyebrow lifts. "Like how to be badass training?"

I let out a chuckle. "Something like that. I know you won't stand for bodyguards following you around, so I'll just learn how to be one myself."

"Mhh... I always loved bodyguard romances," Carla teases.

I press a kiss to her mouth, then I ask, "How's your breathing?"

"I just get a little breathless." She takes a deep breath, then continues, "But other than that, I feel fine."

I move the oxygen mask back over her mouth and nose, then I smile at her.

Placing my hand on her stomach, I say, "With a little luck, we might find out whether Raspberry is a boy or a girl."

"Which are you hoping for?" Carla asks.

Shaking my head, I reply, "As long as Raspberry is healthy, I really don't care."

Carla smiles as she places her hand over mine, then her eyes focus on mine. Emotion washes over her face as she whispers, "I was so scared."

Moving closer to her, I wrap my arms around her. "You and Raspberry are safe now."

Carla nods against my chest.

"I love you," I murmur against her hair.

She lifts her hand to the back of my shoulder, and then her body begins to tremble as she begins to cry. After the trauma she survived, I'm surprised she stayed calm for so long.

I keep pressing kisses to her hair while murmuring words of comfort.

CARLA

After I cried my eyes out, Noah helped me to the bathroom and gave me a sponge bath.

Back in bed and wearing my own clothes, I feel a hell of a lot better.

One hour with Noah and I'm as good as new. That's the power he has over me. It's like he's my life force.

The door opens, and Mrs. West and my parents come in.

Dad comes to kiss my forehead, then he asks, "How do you feel?"

"Like a new person." I smile.

Mrs. West checks the tubes which drain any fluids from my lungs, then she says, "I'll remove the tubes first thing tomorrow morning. Okay?"

I nod, then ask, "Do I still have to use the oxygen mask?"

"Only if you feel you need it."

Her answer makes my smile grow.

Mrs. West gives my hand a squeeze, then she says, "I'm sorry you got hurt…"

I quickly shake my head. "Don't apologize. It wasn't your fault."

The corner of her mouth lifts slightly.

Just then the door opens again, and Dr. Wells comes in. "How's momma and baby doing this afternoon?"

"Good," I answer.

Mrs. West goes to stand at the foot of the bed so Dr. Wells can get to the ultrasound equipment, which I didn't even notice until now.

Noah comes to stand on my left, and when he takes hold of my hand, I link our fingers, giving him an excited smile. Lifting my hand, he presses a kiss to the back of it.

While Dr. Wells neatly pushes my t-shirt up, she says, "You just need to get a lot of rest so your body can heal. Let's see how baby's doing."

She squirts some gel on my skin, then she moves the scanner over my stomach toward my abdomen. A grainy image begins to show, and then my eyes are glued to the screen, even though I can't make out much.

Dr. Wells keeps moving the scanner around until she finds what she's looking for.

When I see a glimpse of Raspberry, I let out a gasp.

Dr. Wells presses harder, and then we see the inside of my womb and Raspberry. Pointing with an arrow, Dr. Wells says, "There's baby's face. Here are the eyes."

My chin begins to quiver as emotion pours through me.

"Oh, there's a foot," Dr. Wells exclaims. "Oops, there was a foot. But those are the legs."

In total awe of our baby, a tear sneaks down my cheek. Noah tightens his grip on my hand.

"Let's look at the gender first before baby changes position," Dr. Wells says. She moves the scanner around until I can't make out what we're looking at. "This is baby's bottom, and that's the femur." She keeps looking, and then she asks, "What are you hoping for?"

"It doesn't matter," I answer quickly.

"Let's see." The image keeps jumping. "There's the bladder. Ahh… there are three white lines right there. You're having a baby girl."

I instantly burst out in tears. Noah leans over me to press a kiss to my temple. When I hear how uneven his breaths are, it's impossible for me to reign in the overwhelming emotions.

"Yay!" Mom cheers. "We have a granddaughter."

Listening to our family's joy, my eyes find Noah's, and when I see the happiness on his face, I know I couldn't love him more than I do at this moment.

He presses a kiss to my mouth, then whispers, "We're having a girl."

I let out a sputter of laughter. "Yeah."

"She's moving," Dr. Wells says, and both Noah and my eyes dart back to the screen. "Oh, look she's waving. Hi, Mommy and Daddy." Dr. Wells lets out a burst of laughter.

"Her hands are all over the place. Look, there are her fingers."

My bottom lip pushes out as my face crumbles from the wonder of seeing our little girl.

"She's healthy, right?" Dad thinks to ask.

"Yes, she's pretty active in there. Let's find her heartbeat," Dr. Wells replies. She twists the scanner, and then she presses a button, and a fast beat fills the air.

"Aww," Mrs. West coos. "Such a strong beat."

"Yeah, it's one-forty-three, which is normal," Dr. Wells says. "One-ten to one-sixty is average," she explains to us.

Dr. Wells continues to point out the spine, and I can see Raspberry's heart beating. It's all so overwhelming, and my emotions are all over the place.

Dr. Wells moves back to Raspberry's legs. "Yeah, it's definitely a girl. We got a real good look there."

I cling to Noah's hand as we finish up.

"I'm very happy with the baby's progress. I'll see you in four weeks. Okay?"

"Thank you, doctor," Noah says, his voice sounding hoarse with emotion.

"Thank you." I can't stop smiling as she leaves.

Noah gives me a hug before he stands back so my mom can get to me.

We all take turns hugging and laughing. It feels like my heart is overflowing with joy.

Now I just want to get better so I can go home with Noah.

Chapter 27

NOAH

The hospital room was damn busy with family and friends dropping by to check on Carla.

Back at Trinity, we walk into her bedroom. I set her hospital bag down by the foot of the bed, then I turn to face her. "Finally, I have my girls all to myself again."

Carla's lips instantly split into a wide smile. "I like that." She wraps her arms around my waist and rests her cheek against my chest. "Now I have to catch up with all the work I missed."

"It will be quick. Get on the bed while I grab my laptop."

"Why yours?" Carla asks.

"I made easy-to-study notes for you."

"Damn, I could've used the help during my senior year," she chuckles.

I get the laptop, then sit down next to Carla, and we both lean back against the headboard. Bringing up the document, I place the device on Carla's lap. "Just read through everything while I unpack your bag."

"Okay."

Getting up, I throw the clothes in the laundry basket, and I place Carla's supplements and toiletries back in her bathroom.

"Are you hungry?"

Carla's eyes snap to mine. "Yes, I'm in the mood for something spicy."

"Chile-braised pork tacos?" I ask. "They're pretty good."

"Yeah! Get me those." Carla thinks for a moment. "And a milkshake. Vanilla."

"I was wondering when the cravings were going to start," I mutter as I take out my phone to order in.

"Ooh, get me a slice of cheesecake, as well," Carla quickly adds.

She watches as I place the order, and when I hang up, she gives me a pleased grin.

"Get to work," I remind her as I drop down beside her again.

Carla reads over the notes for a couple of minutes, then she asks, "Don't you need to study for your finals? You can email the document to me, then I can use my own laptop."

Meeting her gaze, I shake my head. "Nope. I'm good."

Carla pulls a disgruntled face, then she mutters, "So freaking unfair."

"What?"

She lets out a huff. "That you don't even have to study." She turns to face me. "Do you just look at the sentence, and then you remember it?"

I gesture at the laptop. "What page are you on?"

Carla checks. "Page fourteen."

"Pick a line."

She frowns at me, then says, "Uhhh... nine."

"Viability study, which consists of market analysis, technical, financial, and ecological viability."

Carla checks the document then she scowls at me. "That was line eight and nine. Like I said, so freaking unfair." She thinks of something that makes her smile. "I hope Raspberry gets your brains."

I let out a chuckle. "And your looks."

Carla moves the laptop aside, and then she turns to me. "What names do you like for a girl?"

Picking up the laptop, I push it back into her hands. "Work, Carla. When we take a break to eat, we can talk baby names."

She scrunches her nose at me. "No fun."

I tilt my head, and taking hold of her jaw, I press a hard kiss to her mouth. "Work."

She gives me a playful glare before she focuses on the document.

With Carla caught up on the work she missed, I've made a couple of appointments for us to view houses. She's healing nicely, and her baby bump has had a growth spurt, as well.

I'm in a hurry to get out of the suite, and with my finals only two weeks away, I want us in our own house as soon as possible.

After I've parked the car in the driveway, we climb out. Meeting Carla at the front of the vehicle, I link our fingers together before heading to the front door.

Suzanna opens just as we're about to ring the bell. "Hi, guys. I really think you're going to like this one."

"Hi, thanks for showing it to us," Carla says.

"Have a look around. I'll be in the kitchen," Suzanna says, then she gives us our privacy.

From our previous appointments, Suzanna quickly learned to let us explore on our own before she gives us a run down of all the details.

We walk into a spacious living room with large bay windows.

"Lots of light," I murmur.

"I love the layout," Carla says.

We venture through the ground floor, then go upstairs.

The moment we walk into the third bedroom, Carla shrieks, "Yes! This one is perfect. Plenty of closet space and the wide windowsill is just what I wanted. We can arrange all the stuffed animals on it. I can ask Aria to paint raspberries and ladybugs on that wall."

I just stare at Carla as she shares her plans for the room, then she turns to me, asking, "What do you think?"

I shake my head. "That we're probably taking this house before seeing the rest of it?"

She lets out a burst of laughter. "We can fix everything else, but this room needs to be perfect for Raspberry."

"Yeah? So this is the house you want?" I ask to make sure.

Carla gives me a pleading look, which melts my heart. Smiling at her, I do my best to mimic *Olaf* from *Frozen*, "Some people are worth melting for."

Instead of laughing her ass off, Carla slams into me, kissing the living shit out of me. I stumble back against the wall, gripping her tightly so she doesn't fall.

When she breaks the kiss, she murmurs, "If we were at the suite, I'd give you the ride of your life right now."

"I didn't think Olaf would be a turn on for you," I chuckle.

"It's not Olaf. You were cute." She presses another kiss to my lips.

"Cute?" I grumble against her mouth, then I shake my head. "No, I'm never cute." I switch our positions, so Carla's against the wall, and then I remind her why cute is the last word to associate with me.

CARLA

Since the shooting, Noah's been super protective of me, and I'm not going to lie, I love all the attention. Raspberry is growing fast, and at twenty-two weeks, it looks like I swallowed a volleyball.

I tighten my hold on Noah's hand as we walk through the furniture store. We're looking for a lounge suite and entertainment system, then we'll be done with all the purchases for the first floor. I'm leaving Raspberry's room for last.

Suddenly I feel a flutter, and it makes me stop dead in my tracks.

"What's wrong?" Noah asks.

I quickly press his hand to my stomach, and when I feel the flutter again, a wide smile spreads over my face. My gaze darts to Noah. "Did you feel the flutter?"

"Was that Raspberry?" he asks.

I nod, and then we feel her move again. We let out happy chuckles, and then Noah wraps his arm around my shoulders, pressing a kiss to the side of my head. Moving my arm around his lower back, we continue to walk.

It takes us a good twenty minutes to agree on a charcoal leather suite. I leave it up to Noah to decide which entertainment system to get.

The moment we're done, I ask, "Can we have dinner now?"

"Yeah, what are you in the mood for?"

"Pizza and ice cream."

Noah lets out a burst of laughter as we leave the store. After we've had dinner, we head back to Trinity. I can't wait until we can move into our house. Just one more week.

After I've showered, Noah rubs the stretch mark lotion all over my body. When he's done, he lies down behind me and starts pressing kisses to my shoulder and neck.

"What about Catelynn?" I ask as his hand moves between my legs, and he begins to softly caress my clit.

"I'm not feeling it," he murmurs against my neck before he sucks on my skin.

Noah pushes his right arm under my head and wraps it around me. Lifting my hands, I take hold of his forearm as heat pools between my legs.

"Amelia," I breathe while grinding down on his fingers, working their magic on my clit. Noah enters a finger inside me, drawing a moan from me.

The bigger my stomach gets, the gentler Noah becomes in bed. As if he's scared that he'll hurt Raspberry.

It doesn't mean the sex is any less great. Hell no, Noah still blows my mind.

Using his leg, Noah pushes my legs apart, and then I feel his cock at my entrance. He enters me slowly until he's deep inside of me. It feels so good a tremble rushes through my body.

He keeps his thrusts slow and deep, and soon it becomes delicious torture until an intense orgasm seizes my body, drawing a satisfied gasp from me. Then only does Noah speed up, making my release intensify as he finds his own.

When we've both come down from our highs, and Noah pulls out, I say, "I need to pee. Help me up."

Noah lets out a chuckle as he scoops me up in his arms. Carrying me to the bathroom, he sets me down in front of the toilet before he leaves, muttering, "The words every man wants to hear after making his woman orgasm."

I relieve myself while laughing at his comment.

When I'm done, I walk back to the bed, and lying down, I snuggle with the pregnancy support pillow Noah got me.

When Noah's arms wrap around me from behind, he says, "What about Haley? We can nickname her Haleybug, and it kinda rhymes with the ladybugs you want all over the nursery wall."

Glancing over my shoulder, I stare at Noah as I try out the name, "Haley West." A wide smile spreads over my face. "Haleybug. I love it."

"Yeah?" Noah grins at me.

I nod as he leans in to press a kiss to my mouth.

Chapter 28

NOAH

"Carla, where do you want the dresser?" I call out.

She comes into the room, glances around, then points at the wall near the window. "There, please."

Kao and I lift it and carry it to the spot she wants it, then we step back.

"Perfect," she grins at us. "Thanks, guys."

Carla darts back out to finish up in the guest room with Fallon.

All our friends are here today to help us move in, which I'm grateful for, otherwise, I don't know when we'd get it all done.

"So..." Kao begins. "Why didn't you hire a moving company?"

I let out a chuckle as he reminds me of the question I asked him when he and Fallon moved into their home. "Carla wanted to do it this way. If it were up to me, I would've hired a company to help us."

Kao lets out a burst of laughter. "She has you wrapped around her little finger."

I shake my head but then admit, "Yeah, she does."

We walk out of the room and head down the stairs to see what else there is to do.

Forest and Aria are busy in the kitchen, unpacking the sets of plates and cups Carla got.

"Noah?" I hear Carla call.

I move to the entrance, then glance up the stairs. "Yeah?"

"Have you seen the bedside table for the guest room?"

"I'll check down here." Searching, I find it in the dining room and quickly take it to Carla. After setting it down next to the bed, I move to Carla's side. "When are you taking a break?"

"Now," she replies while rubbing her side.

Moving her hand out of the way, I begin to rub her lower back. "You should lie down for a bit. I'll finish up."

"Yeah, Noah's right," Fallon says. "You've been on your feet all day. Go take a nap."

Carla shakes her head. "I'm fine, guys. Besides, we're almost done."

"When are you decorating the nursery?" Fallon asks.

"Aria's going to paint a wall for me. She said it would take her two weeks. I'll wait until then," Carla answers. She lifts a hand to the back of my neck and pulls me down for a kiss before she says, "Let's get back to work. The sooner we're done, the sooner we can relax."

Leaving the women, I go look for Kao. Finding him out front where he's busy placing empty boxes in the U-Haul we hired, I begin to help him.

"Only fourteen weeks to go, right?" Kao asks.

"Yeah."

"Do you have a due date yet?"

"Dr. Wells says Haley should come around May 12th," I answer Kao. "It's just an estimation, though."

After passing my degree with flying colors, my days are filled with working at Indie Ink while my nights are spent with Carla. It feels like we're settling into a routine, and I don't feel so restless anymore.

I glance back at the house we'll call home from now on, a smile curving my lips up.

Things are falling nicely into place.

My gaze moves up to the second floor, and my smile widens when I see Carla staring down at me from the window.

She blows me a kiss before she turns back to whatever she's busy with.

Three years back, something similar happened where I caught Carla watching me from her bedroom window. Then it filled me with apprehension, but now... it fills me with happiness.

It's funny how life throws curveballs that at first seem like the worst possible thing, only to turn out to be the greatest blessing.

Once we settled into our new place, Carla decided it's time to get our parents together for dinner.

So here we are, the kitchen going up in flames and the fire alarm going off because Carla just had to try cooking.

"I've got it," I say as I extinguish the fire.

"My roast," Carla whimpers.

I open the windows and back door so the smoke can get out, and then I turn off the alarm.

Walking to a distraught Carla, I wrap my arms around her and say, "Don't worry. I'll order in. We still have time."

Carla's chin quivers as she glances up at me. "But I wanted to prepare the meal."

"I know." I press a kiss to her mouth. "There's always next time. Okay?" I turn her around and push her out of the smokey kitchen. "Let's draw you a bubble bath, then you can soak and relax while I get everything ready."

Carla nods as I usher her up the stairs to the bathroom. I make sure the water's temperature is right before I press a kiss to Carla's forehead. "Relax. Okay? By the time you're done, I'll have everything ready."

Carla tilts her head, a look of wonder washing over her face. "You're perfect."

The corner of my mouth lift. "Only to you."

She shakes her head. "Nope. You're the closest thing to an angel if I've ever seen one."

I pull her into my arms and press a tender kiss to her mouth. Since the shooting, I find it hard to let her out of my sight. It sent my protective side into overdrive.

It also made me realize Carla is irreplaceable in my life. She fills every heartbeat with happiness and love.

"You're the angel for carrying our child," I murmur. I nudge her toward the tub. "Take your time."

The instant I pull the door shut behind me, I make a run for the kitchen while pulling my phone out of my pocket.

I place an order with a nearby restaurant, and then I begin to clean up the mess. I light scented candles to help clear the smell of smoke from the kitchen.

By the time I'm done in the kitchen, the restaurant delivers our order.

I'm busy opening the containers and transferring the food over to glass bowls when Carla comes back into the kitchen.

"Oh my gosh, Noah. How did you manage to get this done so fast?" Her eyes widen at me. "Do you have superpowers I don't know about?"

I let out a chuckle as I place the food in the oven to keep it warm. "Do you feel better?"

"Yeah. All thanks to you." Carla comes to take my hand, and then she pulls me out of the kitchen. "Your turn to get cleaned up. I'll set the table."

I let out a breath of relief as I head to our bedroom.

As long as Carla's happy, I'm happy.

CARLA

We finished decorating the nursery today and glancing around the room, I'm so happy I could burst.

The ladybug and raspberry theme gives color to everything.

Noah picks up a nursery rhymes book and goes to sit on the rocking chair. Patting his lap, he grins at me.

I carefully position myself on his lap, then wrap my arms around his neck and rest my head on his shoulder.

Noah opens the book to the first rhyme and begins to read. "Humpty Dumpty sat on a wall. I still don't get why an egg would sit on a wall, but okay." He continues to read the rhyme, and it has me letting out a burst of laughter.

When Noah is done reading, he says, "A while back, there was a controversial thing about Humpty Dumpty."

I begin to laugh again, and patting his chest, I mutter, "Why am I not surprised you know that?"

Noah sets the book down, and then he takes hold of my jaw, lifting my face to his. "Yeah, but you still love me."

"With all my heart," I whisper. Staring into his eyes, I think about how far we've come. "To think, a year ago, you wouldn't even talk to me unless you really had to, and now you're reading me nursery rhymes."

Tilting his head, a loving expression softens his features. "Yeah, look at us now."

I let out a chuckle as I brush my fingers through his hair. "I knew you'd end up being mine."

"Yeah? How?" He asks, his hand brushing over my stomach.

"I could just feel it deep in my bones," I admit. "It's like you're ingrained in my heart."

Noah's mouth curves up. "You're the epitome of emotion... of love and life, to me."

His words make emotion flood me until it feels as if it will leak from my eyes.

"I love you, Noah West." Leaning forward, I press my mouth to his, and soon we're lost in a kiss filled with everything we feel.

———————————

Because my due date is in May, the academy is allowing me to speed up my studies so I can write my exams before I go into labor. It means that I've been studying my butt off. Luckily, the notes Noah made for me make it easier to remember everything.

Closing my eyes, I mutter, "Will I even use any of this in the real world?" Haley stretches, and it instantly makes me smile. Rubbing a hand over my stomach, I whisper, "Just eight more weeks, Haleybug."

I hear footsteps come down the hallway, and then Noah walks into the room. He tugs off his tie and drops it on the foot of the bed before he crawls onto the mattress. Leaning over me, he presses a kiss to my mouth.

"How was your day?"

"Okayish," I say, gesturing to the laptop. "How was yours?"

Noah brushes a hand over my stomach, pressing a kiss to it, then he answers, "Long." He drops down beside me, then snuggles into my side. "I just want to shower, eat, and then hold my girls until I fall asleep."

Lifting my hand, my fingers caress the line of his jaw. "Go shower while I get the food ready. We can relax afterward and watch a movie."

Noah pushes himself up again. "Sounds good."

I scoot off the bed and walking to the kitchen, I warm the steaks and vegetables I brought from the campus restaurant. I'll have to learn how to cook at some point, though, but I thought I'd wait until I'm done with my exams.

As I'm placing the plates on the island in the kitchen, Noah comes in. The sweatpants he's wearing hang low on his hips, giving me a yummy view of his abs.

He opens the fridge, asking, "What do you want to drink?"

"A tall glass of you," I mutter. Noah lets out a chuckle, glancing at me from over his shoulder. "Just water is fine."

When we sit down and begin to eat, I notice Noah frowning. It has me asking, "Is everything okay at work?"

Noah swallows the bite he took, then he lets out a sigh. "There's a new receptionist. She started a week ago, and… she just annoys me."

Tilting my head, I set down my cutlery. "Why does she annoy you?" I ask, not wanting to jump to conclusions.

"She's not my assistant, yet every damn morning she brings me coffee. The way she looks at me makes me uncomfortable."

My eyebrows dart up. "Have you told her you're in a relationship?"

Noah shrugs. "Everyone at Indie Ink knows."

"Yeah, but that doesn't mean she knows," I mutter.

Noah's eyes lock with mine. "So I should tell every woman that crosses my path I'm in a relationship?"

I let out a heavy breath. "No, that would sound arrogant." I reach for his hand and give it a squeeze. "I'll bring you lunch tomorrow. Okay?"

A smile tugs at Noah's lips. "That would be great. Saves me from having to deal with her."

"I better not catch her ogling you," I grumble, a possessive twinge in my chest. Then my gaze drops to his chest. "Cause only I get to drool over you."

Noah closes the distance between us, pressing a hard kiss to my mouth, then he murmurs, "I love this side of you. It's a turn on. Finish dinner so I can take you upstairs."

Chapter 29

NOAH

The second there's a knock at my door, I frown. Before I can answer, the door opens, and Olivia walks in with the damn coffee.

If we weren't at work, I'd tell her to go to hell, but now that I'm the director of finance at Indie Ink, it changes how I deal with these things.

She's halfway to my desk when I mutter, "I don't want coffee. Don't bring me any again."

She smiles way too sweetly. "Everyone needs coffee. Besides, I don't mind."

"I mind," I grumble, my frown turning into a scowl.

"I added extra sugar to turn that frown upside down," she almost fucking sings, annoying the shit out of me.

The door to my office opens, and the second my eyes land on Carla, I'm up from behind my desk. I wasn't expecting her until twelve o'clock.

"Ah… you can't just walk in here," Olivia talks down to Carla.

I move to Carla's side, then say, "Olivia, meet my girlfriend, Carla Reyes."

Olivia's eyes widen with shock, and then her face pales. "I'm so sorry, Miss Reyes. It didn't show that Mr. West had an appointment."

Carla tilts her head, a look of warning tightening her features. "You're not his PA, right?"

Olivia quickly shakes her head.

"Then I advise you to return to your desk because this is one ladder you will not be climbing."

Olivia scrambles out of my office, and by some miracle, she doesn't spill any coffee.

I follow after her, and shutting the door, I lock it before I stalk back to Carla. Framing her face, I crash my mouth to hers, and then I show her what a turn on that was.

Carla drops her bag to the floor as I push her back to my desk. Swiping everything to the side, I lift Carla so she can sit on the edge. "I love these dresses," I say as I unzip my pants. "Easy access."

Carla leans back, bracing herself with her hands resting on my desk.

Moving her panties to the side, I enter her with one thrust. My eyes lock on hers as my hips begin to move.

"Harder," Carla gasps, her breath fanning over her parted lips.

I take hold of her thighs to keep her in place, and then I give my girl what she wants until we're both breathless as we come down from our orgasms.

After we've cleaned up in the ensuite bathroom, I wrap my arms around Carla and hold her to my chest. "Thank you."

"Hopefully, that will take care of things for you," she murmurs as she takes hold of my sides. "Otherwise, you'll just have to fire her."

There's a knock at my door. When I unlock and open it, Kao frowns at me. "Why is your door –" His eyes land on Carla. "Oh, hey. I can come back later." Kao turns around and hurries back down the hallway, making me chuckle.

"Kao, it's okay. Come back," I call after him.

Carla sits down on the couch, giving Kao a smile. "I just need a change of scenery, so I'll be studying here today."

Kao lets out a burst of laughter. "Which means Noah won't be getting any work done." He turns his attention to me. "Do you have the budget for the graphics department?"

"Yeah." I turn to my desk, and seeing the mess, I mutter, "I'll email it to you."

Kao begins to laugh. "Yeah, that sounds like a good idea." He walks to the door, and before shutting it behind him, he says, "Enjoy work."

Walking to my desk, I fix everything, and then I ask, "Can I get you anything before I get back to work?"

Carla shakes her head as she opens her laptop. "I'm good."

I take my seat and quickly forward the documents to Kao, then my gaze goes to Carla. Leaning back, I watch as she studies.

"You need to work," she murmurs without looking up.

"With you sitting there looking beautiful, it's hard to focus," I mutter.

Glancing up, she asks, "Should I leave?"

I quickly shake my head and focus my gaze on my work.

CARLA

Noah packs my hospital bag for the hundredth time.

"No matter how many times you do that, the contents will stay the same," I mutter.

"I'm just checking," he grumbles before setting the bag down by the front door. "Let's go over everything again."

I roll my eyes as I lean my head back against the couch. "No, I'm tired."

"Okay, we don't have to act it out. Just run over it with me."

I let out a sigh. "If I feel a contraction or my water breaks, I have to call you no matter where you are." I narrow my eyes at him as he sits down next to me. "Which is kind of a given."

"I'll take the bag, grab the keys, and get you into the car." Then Noah adds, "Calmly."

I give him a look of warning. "When it feels like my vagina is about to tear open, I promise you I will be everything but calm. Prepare yourself for hurricane Carla."

"Probably category five as well," he mutters.

My eyebrows pop up. "Say what?"

Noah's expression quickly turns loving. "Nothing."

"Yeah, that's what I thought," I grumble. "God, she's sitting on my bladder again." I begin to struggle off the couch. Noah helps me to stand before I freaking waddle to the restroom.

Just two more weeks.

When I try to pee, there are only a few drops. Sighing, I frown at my stomach. "Haley, get off Mommy's bladder."

When I walk back into the living room, Noah grins at me. "Feeling better?"

"False alarm," I mumble as I sit down.

He gets up and returns seconds later with my pillow. "Turn sideways and snuggle up."

I do as he says, loving the idea of a nap. Noah sits down next to me, and then he begins to rub my lower back.

"Sorry, I'm so moody," I murmur.

"Don't worry about it." He turns on the TV and puts on *Madagascar*.

After a couple of minutes of watching, I impersonate *Marty*, "As long as we are together, it doesn't matter to me."

"Me too," Noah agrees. "Are you going to teach Haley how to do impersonations?"

"I thought they annoyed you," I say as I close my eyes from the relief I feel in my back.

"I love them," Noah admits.

"Since when?" I mumble half asleep.

"Since it's you doing them," Noah replies.

When I let out a groan, Noah increases the pressure.

"God, that feels good," I moan before I drift off to sleep.

———————

Mom planned a barbeque for the baby shower. It's being held at my parent's place, so there's enough space for everyone.

The house and back yard are brimming with all our friends and family, and as my gaze sweeps over them, I feel blessed.

Even the Hayes' family managed to make it today. Seeing Tristan sitting beside Hana, I wonder when they're going to tie the knot.

Dash and Christopher walk toward me. Noah told me they're just best friends, but I get the same vibes from them that I got from Forest and Aria.

Smiling at them, I say, "Thanks for coming, guys. It means a lot to me."

"I wouldn't dare miss it," Dash replies. She hands me a gift bag. "This is for you."

I peek inside, and then my smile widens. I pull the bracelet out, then Dash explains. "It has the birthstones for each of you as charms." I notice an N, a C, and an H inscribed on the gold leaves where the stones are embedded.

"This is so awesome." Leaning forward, I hug Dash. "Thank you so much." Dash helps me put it on, and then I grin at her. "I love it."

"I thought Mommy deserves something of her own."

"Christopher, you made it," Noah says as he comes to join us.

"Dash threatened my life," Christopher replies. When they shake hands, he asks, "You're taking three weeks off once the baby's born, right?"

Noah nods. "Mr. Reed will fill in for me."

Christopher nods, seeming pleased with the answer.

I hold up my wrist so Noah can see the bracelet. "Look at what Dash gave me."

Noah's lips curve up, then he glances at his sister. "Thanks, Dash."

"I got something for you as well," she says.

Dash hands Noah a gift bag, and I watch as he takes a tiny shirt out. It has '*Always his little girl*' written on the front. Then Noah pulls out another shirt, and my tears instantly tear up when I read, '*Always her hero.*'

"Oh my gosh," I sniffle. "They're perfect."

Dash wraps her arm around me, giving me a sideways hug. "I thought you'd love them."

Chapter 30

NOAH

"Noah!" Carla yells from upstairs.

"Yeah?"

"Noah. Noah. Noah! Oh. My. God."

I drop the cup in the sink and run out of the kitchen and up the stairs. Carla's standing in the middle of the hallway, staring down at a puddle of water.

It takes me a second to realize her water broke.

"Shit, Haley's coming," I shout.

"Yes," Carla chuckles. "Haley's coming."

"Bag." I turn around and run to where we left it by the front door. "Keys." I grab the car keys from the bowl.

Then I hear Carla, "Aren't you forgetting something?"

"Fuck." I dart back up the stairs and taking hold of her arm, I try to move her as fast as possible.

When I have her in the car, she chuckles, "The bag, Noah."

"Shit. Yes." I run back inside and grab the bag.

Then Carla calls out, "Lock the door."

I stop on the stairs, and turning around, I lock the door while taking a deep breath.

Get your shit together, Noah. Stay calm.

When I get in the car, Carla asks, "Should we even be going to the hospital now? The contractions haven't started."

I keep my eyes on the road as I drive away from our house.

"Noah, did you hear me? Shouldn't we wait?" she asks.

"I… I can't remember," I mutter, unable to recall anything I've learned about labor. "My mind's gone blank."

Carla begins to laugh, and it has me glancing at her. "Why are you laughing. What's wrong? Are you okay?" I ramble.

"My going into labor has you totally rattled. I've never seen you like this," she explains.

I glance at her again. "Aren't you nervous?"

"Nope." She let's the fucking 'P' pop. "You have that part all covered."

When we get to the hospital, I begin to breathe a little easier, knowing help is inside. Getting out, I grab the bag, then rush around the front to get Carla.

"Calm down." She takes a deep breath, showing for me to do the same. "We have time."

"I'll calm down when you're inside. Let's go," I mutter as I wrap my arm around her shoulders.

Once we have Carla settled in the private room, I slump down on the couch and take a deep breath.

Carla shakes her head at me. "I'll probably have to keep you calm while giving birth."

"Sorry," I say as I get up. I walk to the bed and sit down next to her. "I'll be calm."

Miss Sebastian comes into the room. "I heard my grand-god-baby is coming."

"How?" I shake my head. "We've only been here ten minutes."

"My bedazzled ass knows everything." She places her hand on Carla's shoulder. "How do you feel?"

"Excited," Carla replies, a wide smile on her face.

"No contractions yet?" Miss Sebastian asks.

Carla rubs over her stomach as she answers, "Not that I know of. I told Noah we should've waited before coming in."

"You're here now. Make yourself comfortable. It might take a while," Miss Sebastian says, then she walks to the door. "Let me know if you need anything."

"You'll probably know before we do," I mutter, but she's already out the door.

———————————

Carla started having contractions four hours ago, and they're beginning to grow with intensity.

Carla just sits with her eyes closed as if she's meditating while the contraction passes. When her eyes open, I murmur, "I love you. Thank you for doing this."

"Love you, too." She gives me a smile before reaching for her ice water, then she begins to scoot off the bed. "I need to move around."

I quickly dart to my feet and hover behind her as she begins to pace, then Carla stops and glances at me from over her shoulder. "You can sit."

"Okay." I keep standing, though. It's as if my body is wired to respond to everything Carla does.

She's just about to walk by me when her hand darts out, and she grabs hold of my arm. "Shit."

I move closer and rub my hand over her lower back, wishing there was more I could do.

Carla begins to whimper, and it fucking breaks my heart.

"I'm going to throw up," she groans. I dart for the pan. "Hurry, hurry." I make it just in time as Carla loses all the fluids I managed to get into her.

When she's done, I go empty it in the toilet before rinsing the pan with some mouthwash I got from the hospital's drug store.

I set the pan back in its place for when she needs it again. "Are you okay?"

She nods as she slowly walks to the bathroom to rinse out her mouth.

Time crawls by as the contractions come faster.

Miss Sebastian comes into the room. "Are you okay with me assisting with the birth?"

"Hell yeah," I answer before Carla can respond.

"Please," Carla breathes through another contraction.

"Great, let's see how far you're dilated."

I help Carla back on the bed, and when Miss Sebastian is done checking, she grins at us. "We're good to go. Let's start doing some practice pushes. Okay?"

Carla nods, and my heart begins to beat faster.

Miss Sebastian helps Carla into position, and then she says, "Take a deep breath, and then you push as hard as you can for ten seconds."

Carla sucks in a deep breath of air, and then she begins to push while Miss Sebastian counts to ten.

Seeing the strain Carla is under makes me feel helpless as fuck. Not knowing what else to do, I say, "You're doing great."

Carla lets out the breath she's been holding with a cry.

"Let's do another," Miss Sebastian orders.

Carla shakes her head. "No. Wait. I need a minute."

I wet a cloth in icy water, and after squeezing the excess fluid out, I pat it over Carla's forehead. "The back of my neck, " she murmurs. I've just placed the cloth there when she groans, "I'm going to be sick. Quick."

I grab the pan wondering where the hell all this fluid is coming from, seeing as she hasn't had anything else.

It feels as if everything is on repeat for the next hour, and then finally, Dr. Wells is called.

"Okay, Mommy, it's time to push as hard as you can," Dr. Wells says as she sits down in front of Carla.

Not knowing what to do with myself, I link my fingers behind my neck as I watch Carla push with everything she has.

Miss Sebastian grabs hold of my arm and yanks me to the foot of the bed, and then my mouth drops open as a sensation strips me bare. It's a mixture of amazement, pride, and the most intense love I've ever felt.

My eyes keep darting between Carla's face and Haley's head.

Carla lets out a cry as she gives one last push, and then everything blurs as tears flood my eyes. I dart back to Carla's side, and framing her face, I press a kiss to her parted lips. Pulling back, I don't care that she's seeing me cry as I say, "I love you so much. I'm so proud of you."

Carla catches her breath as she looks down, and then she begins to cry as her gaze locks on Haley.

"You have a healthy baby girl. Congrats," Dr. Wells says while Miss Sebastian cleans Haley. She wraps her in a blanket then comes to lay her in Carla's arms.

Seeing the woman I love holding my baby girl is unbelievable. For a moment, I can only stare before I lean over them. I press a kiss to Carla's forehead then murmur, "She's beautiful. Just like her Mom."

Carla smiles up at me, and then she says, "Hold your daughter, Daddy."

My stomach begins to churn with nerves as Carla places Haley in my arms. "Hey, my Haleybug," I murmur. I try to memorize every inch of my baby girl while my heart splits in two – one half belonging to Carla and the other to Haley.

CARLA

We've been home two days, and sitting in the rocking chair, I'm breastfeeding Haley. Noah's seated between the stuffed animals on the windowsill, his eyes constantly darting between my face and Haley.

"What are you thinking?" I ask.

The corner of his mouth lifts. "That I want to marry you."

I begin to blink, not sure I heard right.

Noah realizes what he said, and darting from the windowsill, he comes to crouch next to the chair. His gaze locks with mine. "Will you? Marry me?"

Emotion pushes up my throat as I nod like a crazy person. "Yes. Definitely yes."

He shoots up, and framing my face, he presses a hard kiss to my mouth before he pulls back to look at me. "Want to go look at rings? I wasn't expecting to ask you like this, so I'm not prepared."

I let out a chuckle. "I'd like that."

"I'll make it up to you," he says before giving me another kiss.

Shaking my head, I murmur, "This was perfect."

When Haley's had enough, I burp her before she falls asleep.

"Go get dressed while I check Haley's bag," Noah says, nudging me out of the nursery.

I go to our bedroom, and stripping out of the sweatpants and shirt I was wearing, I put on a dress. I fix my hair and swipe on some lipgloss before I search for my sandals.

Finding them half under the bed, I slip them on, then head back to the nursery. When I walk inside, I pick up Haley so we can leave.

"We're only going for the ring, right?" I ask as we head to the car.

"Yeah, unless you want to do something else while we're out?"

I strap Haley in her car seat, and then Noah double checks me. "We can get some takeout then spend the rest of the day watching movies?"

"Whatever you want to do," Noah murmurs as we climb in the car.

I expected things to be crazy once Haley was born, but it's been calm. Noah and I take turns changing the diapers, and with Haley sleeping from eleven at night through to five in the morning, we both get our rest, as well.

"We're so lucky. I've read horror stories about babies never sleeping and things just being insane the first couple of months," I mention.

"Yeah, she's amazing," Noah agrees as he steers the car down the road.

When we get to Tiffany's & Co, my heartbeat speeds up, and excitement builds in my chest. Only when I'm staring at the engagement ring collection does it set in.

Noah asked me to marry him.

We're busy choosing a ring.

I lift a hand to cover my mouth as I gasp, and then my eyes dart to him. "Oh. My. God."

Worry instantly blooms over his face, and he stops rocking the stroller. "What's wrong?"

My eyes tear up as I whisper, "You asked me to marry you."

Noah begins to laugh as he pulls me to his chest. Pressing a kiss to my hair, he mutters, "I wondered why you were so calm."

Wrapping my arms around his waist, I bury my face against his chest as the overwhelming emotions rush through me.

"Is everything okay?" A store assistant asks behind me.

"Yes," Noah replies, rubbing his hand over my back.

I pull away and quickly wipe the tears from my cheeks as I take deep breaths. Smiling at the assistant, I explain, "He asked me to marry him less than an hour ago, and it only sunk in now."

"Awww…" the lady coos.

When I look at the rings again, it only heightens my emotions. I choose a round brilliant center stone with a diamond platinum band designed by the late Jean Schlumberger.

The assistant measures my ring finger, and then she smiles. "It's the right size, so we don't have to get it fitted."

Noah takes over so he can pay while I check to make sure Haley's still off in dreamland.

The second we're in the car, I yank my phone out and dial Mom's number.

"Hi, sweetheart," Mom answers.

307

I begin to sob. "Mom, Noah asked me to marry him!"

There's a moment's silence, and then Mom shrieks, "Ahhhhh… I'm so happy for you! That's the best news."

I try to control my breathing as I ramble, "I just wanted to tell you. We just bought the ring. I'll call you later so we can chat."

"Okay, sweetheart. Congratulations. Enjoy every second."

Once I've ended the call, I turn to Noah and throw myself at him. Pressing kisses all over his face, I say, "I. Love. You. So. Much."

Noah begins to laugh. "I love you. Let's get home because I'm sure as fuck not screwing this up more by putting the ring on your finger in the car."

I feel like I'm high, and by the time we get home, I'm buzzing with excitement. The instant Noah places Haley down in her bed, I say, "Show me. Show me. Show me."

He chuckles as he pulls the box from his pocket, and when he opens it, I let out a weird sound, something between a sob and a laugh.

"Carla." My eyes snap to Noah's. "I never thought the little girl with her pigtails who used to annoy the living hell out of me would become the woman I can't live without.

You've shown me more happiness than I've experienced in my entire life. Will you marry me?"

Unable to say anything, I nod like crazy while holding my right hand out to him.

"Other hand," Noah chuckles.

I let out a burst of laughter as I quickly switch hands, and when Noah pushes the ring on my finger, everything stills in me.

This is the moment I dreamt of for so many nights. This is what I wanted more than anything.

My chin quivers as I look up at Noah. "You've always been my world." I glance down at Haley. "Now you've given me the universe."

Noah presses a kiss to my mouth, and then I impersonate *Buzz Lightyear*, "To infinity and beyond."

Noah begins to chuckle. "I knew you were going to say that. You couldn't resist the urge, could you?"

"Nope."

The End.

Want to read where it all started?

Go 1 Click HEARTLESS.

And when you're done with the Enemies To Lovers Series,

follow it up with Trinity Academy.

All the sale links are listed in the back matter of the book.

The Heirs

Reading order of future releases:

Coldhearted Heir
Novel #1
Hunter Chargill (*Mason and Kingsley's son*)
&
Jade Daniels (*Rhett & Evie's daughter*)

Arrogant Heir
Novel #2
Jase Reyes – (*Julian & Jamie's son*)
&
Mila West – (*Logan & Mia's Daughter*)

Defiant Heir
Novel #3
Kao Reed (*Marcus and Willow's son*)
&
Fallon Reyes (*Falcon & Layla's daughter*)

Loyal Heir
Novel #4
Forest Reyes (*Falcon & Layla's son*)
&
Aria Chargill (*Mason & Kingsley's daughter*)

Callous Heir
Novel #5
Noah West (*Jaxson & Leigh's son*)
&

Carla Reyes (*Julian & Jamie's daughter*)

Sinful Heir
Novel #6
Tristan Hayes (*Carter & Della's son*)
&
Hana Cutler (*Lake & Lee's daughter*)

Tempted Heir
Novel #7
Christopher Hayes (*Carter & Della's son*)
&
Dash West (*Jaxson & Leigh's daughter*)

Forbidden Heir
Novel #8
Ryker West (*Logan & Mia's son*)
&
Danny Hayes (*Carter & Della's daughter*)

A spin-off Stand-Alone
(from Coldhearted Heir and
The Trinity Academy series)

Not My Hero

Colton Lawson
(*Brady's brother*)
&
Brie Weinstock
(*Serena Weinstock's daughter*)

Trinity Academy

FALCON
Novel #1
Falcon Reyes & Layla Shepard

MASON
Novel #2
Mason Chargill & Kingsley Hunt

LAKE
Novel #3
Lake Cutler & Lee-ann Park

JULIAN
Novel #4
A Stand Alone Novel
Julian Reyes (*Falcon's Brother*)
&
Jamie Truman (*Della's Sister – Heartless, TETLS*)

THE EPILOGUE
A Trinity Academy Novella

Enemies To Lovers

Heartless
Novel #1
Carter Hayes & Della Truman

Reckless
Novel #2
Logan West & Mia Daniels

Careless
Novel #3
Jaxson West & Leigh Baxter

Ruthless
Novel #4
Marcus Reed & Willow Brooks

Shameless
Novel #5
Rhett Daniels & Evie Cole

False Perceptions
Novel #6
A Stand Alone Novel
Hayden Cole *(Evie's Dad)*

Connect with me

Newsletter

FaceBook

Amazon

GoodReads

BookBub

Instagram

Twitter

Website

About the author

Michelle Heard is a Wall Street Journal, and USA Today Bestselling Author who loves creating stories her readers can get lost in. She resides in South Africa with her son where she's always planning her next book to write, and trip to take.

Want to be up to date with what's happening in Michelle's world? Sign up to receive the latest news on her alpha hero releases → NEWSLETTER

If you enjoyed this book or any book, please consider leaving a review. It's appreciated by authors.

Acknowledgments

Tayla, thank you for keeping me calm and for taking care of everything while I write.

To my alpha and beta readers, Donita, Taylor, Sherrie, Sheena, Allyson. Kelly, Elaine, Sarah, and Leeann – Thank you for being the godparents of my paper-baby.

Candi Kane PR - Thank you for being patient with me and my bad habit of missing deadlines.

Sybil – Thank you for giving my paper-babies the perfect look.

To my readers, thank you for loving these characters as much as I do.

A special thank you to every blogger and reader who took the time to take part in the cover reveal and release day.

Love ya all tons ;)

Made in United States
Troutdale, OR
11/18/2024

24991744R00177